THE MYSTERY OF MITSUKI

A WERE-TALE

Colleen Sanchez

COPYRIGHT

This is a work of fiction. Names, characters, brands, places, media, and incidents are either the product of the author's imagination or are used fictitiously. The author acknowledges the trademark owners of various products, brands, and/or stores referenced in this work of fiction, which have been used without permission. The publication /use of these trademarks is not authorized, associated with, or sponsored by the trademark owners. All rights reserved. No part of this book may be reproduced or used in any manner without the express written permission of the publisher, except for the brief quotations in a book review.

A young woman, Mitsuki Takeda, is a brilliant and studious yet reclusive girl, who was born in the United States but taken and raised in Japan. She finds herself in a pensive situation when a group of people starts to follow her, not knowing if this group means her harm, she finds herself on the run to her destiny. This girl also is slapped in the face with the reality that one would think only to be a fantasy. When she meets a young man named Shirou and his Naito two brothers, who are also very mysterious with secrets of their own, they will have to unlock the mysteries and secrets that lie deep within her.

CONTENTS

ACKNOWLEDGMENTS

To my mom for being helpful and inspiring through my life and my writing. Plus, always looking out for me.

To my children and husband for putting up with me during my long nights and days and constant questioning while trapped in my creative bubble of doom.

1

TRAVELER

Hi, my name is Mitsuki; I am 20 years old and was born in America. I was brought to Japan by my adoptive parents who originally are from Japan and raised here. I gained my name, Takeda Mitsuki, but I totally still look like I'm American (which I guess technically I still am), not that I have any control of my appearance.

I have reddish blonde hair, which nearly holds a pink tent of color to it. My eyes are deep green; I am exceptionally light complected. I am very short in height but definitely have no issues of holding my own.

It was late in the summer, the weather was sultry, and the sun was beaming down on me as I walked down a deserted street; it had been for several weeks now. Well, I only stopped when I needed to rest. Every now and then, I would stay in a hotel for a night to clean up when I went to a town.

I was swinging my arms as I walked freely, had a pleasant smile, not really looking around much humming a little tune as I continued through the dense forest. I walked into some resting birds. As I got closer to them, they began to pick-up flight all around me out of my path. I was slightly startled a little by the birds' quick movement, letting out a small yelp and grabbing at my chest as I looked at the birds thinking to myself how weird their behavior was.

I continued to watch them flying erratically, rubbing at my brow, and letting out a sigh from my lips. I watched as they flew further and further away. "Well, I wonder what that was all about?" Quietly questioning myself with an annoyed tone since they nearly gave me a small attack.

I turned around to see no one else around me. Letting out another little sigh and continued to walk on south towards Shizuoka, since I was not sure where it was, I was basically just following where my feet led me.

I could hear what sounded like dogs barking and growling in the distance, not seeing any civilization nearby. I was just hoping they weren't a pack of wild dogs. I didn't have the energy to be dealing with that at the moment, also hoping to avoid them, I looked through the trees as I passed by the noises trying not to make noises and drawing attention to myself.

As I made it past them, I thought I almost couldn't remember why I had even started to go this long, the endless walking; however, I was always reminded about the witches as I just kept moving and following where my feet will lead me. I knew that I could not risk going back and refused to get caught by them.

The sun was slowly starting to set in the distance; looking up in the sky, noticing it glowing a bit dim, I kept walking, not bothered by the lateness of the day. You could tell I was tired of it; I am quite sure it showed on my face by now.

My smile started to fade as it grew even darker; I became more interested in my surroundings, looking up at the sky, running my fingers through my wavy hair. "Wonder what is to become of me now? I have lost everything, EVERYTHING!!" letting a series of sighs out as I kneel dramatically to the ground.

"What is it you want from me!?" I yelled out while raising my fists upwardly in the sky. "Oh well, it's not like you were going to come down here personally and tell me.... well WHATEVER!!" I yelled to no one in particular.

Now being nearly pitch-black, no lights and the stars would show if it were not for the slight overcast. "It's been three days, three days, and nothing to show for it. Now I am furthest from everything that I have ever been before." I said again to the open air.

Looking around as I spot a small group of bushes, I then take off my coat, laying it down over the bushes.

I knelt onto the coat laying my head on to it, looking upward, not seeing anything, only hearing the small nightingales bounce around in the trees singing melodies as it grew later and later in the night. My eyes began to close slowly, and I was fast asleep.

Awoken by a mixture of events as the sun rose, the birds and other animals began stirring, making noises, and knocking things down from the trees that were above me.

I looked up, rubbing my eyes then rolling over, trying to wrap my coat over my face letting out an annoyed whine as I tried to cover more; I than rolled over again, wrapping the coat over my face trying to go back asleep.

As I rolled the second time, I could see something in the small opening of my coat, at first. It was still only a blur, and then as my eyes adjusted and began to focus, I could then see denim material. It was only inches away from my face as I quickly sat up, now seeing the full image—a young man looking down at me with a smirk on his face.

••Shirou••

"I can't believe that I am now going back home; it's been a few years while I have been out on different "jobs" my family has been waiting for me to come back for a while now. When I say family, I can confidently say that ours is a pretty big one since mainly we inhabit most of Shizuoka. We are tucked away from outsiders, and we appreciate our seclusion, not liking prying eyes on our families' secrets that could be considered a curse depending on the individual.

I am next in line to inherit the leading role in our family 戦士オオカミパック The Senshi Okami no Mure (warrior pack) as the Alpha, and I'm not really looking forward to it. To be honest, I would be ecstatic if my uncle would just take over, but that is not how it works.

Therefore I am doomed to take the lead when my father steps down. Thankfully that shouldn't be for a while now. So, I'm coming back to my sister Giana (who my mom names after she had a dream about having a daughter named after some French actress), my younger brother Akifumi and my dad Naito Hideaki.

My aunts, uncles, tons of cousins, no nephews or nieces as of yet since my siblings nor I have yet to find our 運命の愛 Mono no unmei no ai (one's destined love).

Wish I could say I was going to see my mom again soon too; however, she died not too long after my brothers birth by some asshole rogues that found their way in our hideaway coming in our home when my father and I were out in Osaka dealing with 黒ムーン the Kuro Mun

Okami no Mure (Black Moon pack).

There are at least five packs spread out in the Japan region, many like ours are hidden away in the deep forests of Japan for a good reason. Luckily, my sister and a baby brother, who was only three at the time, was with one of our aunts.

So us wolves as well as the Kyuketsuki (vampires) and Majo (witches) demons, ghosts, yokai, obake, yurei, and other legendary creatures that are crawling about around humans while some remain clueless, others just try and wish us away with charms and prayers.

I have met a few who have been attempting to learn of us, but it has never worked out for either them or us.

Occasionally there are promised or destined ones that will end up another species, which is uncommon but does tend to happen with humans, witches, vampires, and of course, werewolves; sometimes yokai, obake, yurei, and demons are known to take humans, witches, and sometimes werewolves away on their own because of their own obsessions not because of the natural pull the rest of us have for a mate.

Some beliefs that the reason of this pull is because of a god or goddess of the moon Tsuki Yomi or as the Greeks name her Σελήνη

(Selene).

Whatever the reasons we have, this is what we have to look forward to as some at the age of 16 have been recorded as the earliest to find their mate.

So, I am walking like a crazy wolf from Nara back to Shizuoka; if I weren't on all fours, then it would take me 3 to 4 days to get to Shizuoka, but fortunately, I'm able to shift as long as I keep my head low since humans don't consider Wolves to be a natural setting in Japan.

Our regular wolves in the area have been extinct for many generations; however, there had been "sightings" of wolves still around, but that would be just us as we try not to draw too much attention in our Wolf form. As I make it into our territory, it is getting darker.

I'm carrying a bag in my mouth full of papers of different treaties with the Kiba Okami no Mure (fang pack) in Nara, as well as my clothing for when I shift back to human form.

I'm moving relaxed now, not much in a hurry since I have been traveling for a day and a half, the sun has already set, and so it is getting dark fast. Moving between the trees and over rocks, the wind softly blows through my coat. I can catch a scent that I feel doesn't belong.

It is a fascinating mixture of cherry blossoms, hyacinth, and a sweet musk blended in. Following the smell, I slowly approach a girl who definitely does not belong here; she is lying down.

First, I wasn't so sure if she was alive or not until I see her cloth that she is covered in; her chest moves slightly smoothly, rising and falling as she breathes. I was going to turn around and walk away but had the urgency to stay and get closer to the girl.

So slowly, I moved even closer to her. I placed my bag down and circled around her to see her more closely. I nudged her shoulder with my nose; as I did this, I felt a powerful sensation go through my body.

Definitely thinking this is impossible for me to find my mate in the woods as I am coming home in such a place it was unheard of. I couldn't place her anywhere, not knowing who she was or why she was here, right at this moment. I wanted to waken her but thought better of it as she was sleeping, and I didn't want to scare her away. So, I did the next best thing I could think of and decided to watch over her as she slept so nothing would bother or harm her.

It puzzled me why she was so relaxed in the first place to be sleeping out in the wooded area with only a coat that didn't seem to be thick and a bag of her own; well, it was scorching out and only starting to cool as the sun had set.

I couldn't make out her features too much for she was cuddled tightly in her coat, but I could definitely tell she was petite, and I could make out the little reddish tuffs of her hair peeking out of her coat. I slowly lowered myself next to her and quietly watched her as she slept. Her breathing was rhythmic, and relaxing listening to it calmed me and found myself sleeping as well.

••Third Person POV••

As the birds and other animals began stirring, making noises, and knocking things down from the trees that were above them, he looked up just as some twigs and leaves were falling near his head. He grabbed his bag in his mouth, creeping behind a thicket of trees, shifting into his human form, he holds some jeans out of his pocket and puts them on as well as a grey shirt.

Picking up the bag, he slowly returns to the girls' side as he sees her start to move slowly. It seems as though the animals were disturbing her sleep. He began to get excited, knowing that she would get up, and he would get to meet her finally. After watching her for most of the night, he was genuinely growing more and more impatient for her to get up. Standing close to where she was laying, he looked down at her, watching as she started to roll from one side to the other. Shirou was surprised to see that she was not of local decent. Seeing the foreign girl laying in the ground and knowing she was his mate was unexpected; even so, he found her to be beautiful with her flawless ivory skin and light reddish hair that was wrapped crazily around her face and neck.

She was smiling down as he heard her make small whining noises as she didn't want to awaken, then seeing her jet up in a sitting position and looking rather startled by his presence. He was smirking at her finding her ridiculously cute at that moment. Her hair was askew, some of it sticking to her face from where she was lying on it.

He could see her deep and dark green eyes that seemed to go on forever like the forest around them, feeling like he was being dragged in by force and getting lost in them. She slowly started to stand and had a peculiar expression on her face, ones like bewilderment and slight interest not seeming afraid at all. All he could think of was how lucky he was that she was brave and strong, for why would the weak be in her position?

2

ACQUAINTANCE... GETTING TO KNOW YOU

••Mitsuki••

"Are you ok there?" The young man asks me, still looking up at him, I rose to my feet slowly, not saying a word but keeping my eyes on him. Not particularly afraid of him but not sure about what to think of him either.

He didn't seem to mean me any harm; as the wind started whipping around us, my eyes widened as I could now smell a blend of vetiver and musk with a hint of citrus. Feeling an absolute pull, I felt myself moving towards him as he stood still looking down at me.

I felt as though I had been enlightened to a degree the beast within striving to get out, realizing how close I had come up to the strange young man, I then stepped back just a step to regain control of myself, still watching him closely for I found my feelings very confusing toward him.

He was nicely dressed in afternoon wear,

subtle jeans, and a T-shirt with a satchel over his shoulder. He tilted his head, still standing in the same spot looking at the grass that had stuck on to my mid-length skirt and blouse.

My hair was slightly askew, and I still had leaves and loose grass pieces in my hair. I ran my fingers through my hair, rustling it a bit, trying to straighten it out. Letting my hands fall to my side slowly as he reached over and pick some of the remaining pieces of grass out of my hair, then running the back of his hand on the side of my face, gasping softly, I turned away in embarrassment.

My face sported a cute tint of red as I stepped further away from him. "Are you ok? May I ask your name, miss?" He gently asked. His voice sounded of concern and not harsh at all.

I thought of how my father sounded with harshness; although he was hardly aggressive, just his tone came out extremely strict like, but this man's voice was gentle and sweet, making me purr inwardly. I looked up at him with a blank stare only for a short moment, then blinking a little smiling I then started to speak softly.

"My name is Takeda...Mitsuki," I fell quiet once more, as he could do no more than smile at me, taking in my soft sweet voice sounding so much like an angel to him.

"I see, well, my name is Shirou; it's nice to meet you," unable to stop smiling at me, he grunted softly. Nodding now, I looked to him, bending over some to pick up my coat and bag. I shook out the coat and folded it up in my arms.

As he kept watching me, he noticed me looking in his direction; he thought he'd try and get more information out of me as he had so many questions to ask me. "So, what brings you to Shizuoka?" He started asking in an interested tone.

"Oh. Is that where I am? I have been walking for a long while now, I haven't been to a lot of places 'til now." I said in a carefree way, not with many expressions at all, which confused him a little.

He listened to me; his smile faded into a straight line. Was he concerned as to why I would even be walking out like this at all? He was also noticing my slight accent while I spoke, knowing that I wasn't local, not only from my appearance, which was obvious but my way of speaking was not local at all, either.

"So, your name is Mitsuki? Where are you from? You don't look Japanese, yet you speak so well, and you carry a Japanese name?" I looked at him and smiled, nodding her head. "Yes, I do, all my life now I have had my name," I said in a sing-song voice.

"You see, I was born in America but was raised in Seto Naika and outside of Ozumimachi," I said in a matter of fact tone. His brow raised as he listened to my explanation.

"Oh...I see, well that is interesting." He said, nodding his head. I only smiled then asking my own line of questions to him.

"So, you have a family name, don't you? Shirou?" He laughed a little and nodded his head. "Yes, and it is Naito. So Mitsu, Uhm... it is ok to call you this?"

I looked at him, blushing slightly to the new name he had given to me, and nodded my head, thinking if it is him, then yes, it will be fine. He smiled and continued to talk with me, now inviting me over to eat some breakfast since I was close to his home.

"I can fix you some food. You see, I don't live that far from here, and technically you are already on my family's land. I was starting to wonder if this was the family I was supposed to meet. He's smiling a toothy smile as he looks towards me, hoping I would accept the invitation.

"Oh, w..well Uhm... I'm not sure; I guess so... as I say so, my damn stomach talks louder than me and has already made up its mind as it was growling in protest of not having food, at the slightest mentioning of food even though I was about to deny the request my stomach growls angrily again.

My face was crimson in embarrassment from the betrayal of my stomach; I tried laughing it off. He, too, began laughing along with me. "I guess you better, or you will have to answer to that." He said jokingly, lightly poking at my stomach.

I felt a small piece of me die in embarrassment; my face felt super-hot as I covered my face nodding my head in a friendly fashion.

"I really am sorry I didn't realize anyone lived nearby... I'm sorry." He shook his head and waved it off. "No worries, it's been a long time since we had anyone here."

He helped me up some of the pathways it had rocks that started to roll down as we walked up the incline; as we continued up the hill, I began to see a little short fence it seems really long as it wrapped around a beautiful yet rustic manor. It was huge, tall as it was long.

My eyes widened as they walked a bit closer; it looked like a small community facing him. Meeting my eyes with his, he smiles back down at me. "Well, this is it, we have many homes around this quarter of the property then further back, there are plenty more; this one is the main manor he states as he points to the large home, which is nearly three and a half stories high not counting the attic.

"The head of the family lives here that would be my grandparents, father, brother, and sister too. Some of my cousins are in and out with their ma... or uhm with their spouses." He tried to say slyly (not understanding my situation as to why his mate did not recognize him, and his Wolf seemed to have trouble connecting with hers).

He broke his eyes away from me, scratching the back of his neck nervously. "So, my grandfather is Naito Usaki, who is usually the head of the home when my father is away. My home is past the main house if you would like to get some food in you?" I just looked at him and then back at the collection of homes that were neatly preserved.

They seemed very warm and cozy; as they walked around the main manor towards his house through the opening of small gates still snug against the walls of the main manor, I could finally see it passed the walls and see so many homes on the land.

I had a feeling there were too many even to count. "Uh, you live here, and all these homes belong to your family!? He smiled, looking down at her and nodding quite proudly, gently guiding me to his home.

As they turned another corner and crossed a small path, he faces his humble abode, stopping in front of the house, pointing to the door, he states that they have arrived at his home. It was a modest home with a large tree on the corner with wildflowers growing below it in a ring around the base of the tree.

There were signs that children must play near it with toys scattered like a soccer ball and a couple of nets and a basketball on the grass. It made me smile and feel a little more comfortable seeing there must be children nearby in the small development.

I loved children and loved watching them play and used to watch over them back when I was at home. My eyes seemed hazy as I finally broke from my view from the tree and back at him and then back at home, slightly impressed.

"And you have a wife?" He didn't seem bothered by my question; just let out a gentle sigh as he stopped walking again and looked at me "uh, well, no, I haven't been married. Kind of travel too much right now to be thinking of such things. I was on my back from Nara when I saw something, or should I say someone lying on the ground." Smirking to himself and turned more towards her.

"I was thrilled to see you move. I really

thought you to be yet another tragedy in the woods that we hear about but never experience, especially in our quiet area. I'm happy that wasn't the case. Smiling as he opened the door for me to walk in.

"Please do come in, I know you don't know me, but at least you can clean up and eat while you are here." At that moment, I had a rush of noises starting to surround me. I looked all around me, not seeing anything as I even turned around looking, which Shirou overlooked as he was busy opening windows with his back to me.

I became weak as the noises became more noticeable as the voices that would continue to encircle me. I then started to lose consciousness and hit the floor as he turned back around towards me; seeing me on the ground, he frowned at me, not knowing what had happened.

••Shirou••

He panicked, looking around seeing that no one else was around, he leaned down and picked her up in his arms, her long hair brushing up against his face it felt light and soft like feathers. She looks as peaceful as he carried her back into the living room, placing her softly on the futon.

He walked to the kitchen area, thinking he would put a cold damp cloth for her. After wetting a clean cloth, he brought it back to her as she was still sleeping, placing the cloth on her forehead 'til she came through. Suddenly his phone began to ring.

He walked over to the telephone, and thoughts still ran through his head on what he needed to do; as he picked up the phone, he didn't hear anything.

"Hello Naito residents, how may I help you?" He said in a shaky tone. He suddenly hears someone on the other end of the line.

"Naito residents!? Who are you trying to fool with such efficiency...??" He hears his sister on the other end and sighs in annoyance.

"Ah, yes, Giana, how are you today?" He asks as he is cut off immediately by her.

"Don't try to play me like some fool, what's going on over there; why are you talking so funny!?"

"Ahh... it's nothing, so let me talk with you later... I got to go get some stuff done around here. I haven't been home that long, and you're already giving me a hard time? Just let me unwind before lashing out at me, jeez!! I have a lot on my mind without having to listen to you being ridiculous and harassing me all the time about how officiant I am on the damn phone. I really have to go now, ok??"

He let out a sigh, still hearing her on the other end. "Goodbye then, my goodness, what a drama queen!" Scratching the back of his head, "goodbye, Sis, I will call you when I get settled, ok??"

She quickly yells back at him, and he then hears the dial tone indicating that the call was over. He hung up the phone and ran his fingers through his hair, letting another sigh escape his lips. He had almost forgotten about Mitsuki, who was still lying unconscious on the futon.

He then hurried back to the kitchen, chilling up another small cloth, and went to the living room. She was still not moving as he knelt beside her taking off the now warm cloth and replacing it with the cool one.

He softly wiped her face with the other cloth. She had dirt still on her face from traveling; he was concerned for her and felt lost on what he could do for her. She was so beautiful to him, just so quiet, he wondered if this was her true nature or what was she really like??

Now that they were still and he could see all of her looking down, he could definitely see that she was a westerner for sure all features; he was just surprised by her height; he had thought they were taller and had a thicker stature, but here she was very petite and perfect to him.

She could not have been any taller than 153cm or so compared to his 188cm stature, with him being a mixture of Korean and Japanese descent and being an Alpha. His brother is not as tall as he is at only 166cm, and his sister is about 155cm tall.

He placed the cloth down and decided that he would take her shoes and stockings off so that she would be more comfortable; he got up and placed them by the front door on a small shoe rack. He still wanted to know where she was going with only a small bag in tow; he dares not look inside it though it might let him learn more about her if he did.

"Wise not to go prowling in other things, especially if the other is a female." He stayed to himself knowingly. Just thinking if it were his sisters' bag and he went snooping, it would be the end of his life, no doubt.

He laughed to himself then walked back to her, kneeling beside Mitsuki taking the cloth off her head and turned it around so that the warmth was taken away from her head. He moved her hair around a little, straightening it is looking at her lightly petting her hair.

Shirou began to call her name softly in hopes that she would wake up, but he didn't want to startle her. She was still out cold; it had been at least an hour since he had laid her down on the futon. He was starting to really worry, although her breathing was steady, and she was not too warm. Shirou decided it would be best to call the pack's doctor, who luckily was his uncle.

3

EVER SO CLOSE

••Sasume••

Listening to the radio, Sasume hears the phone start to ring and turns to the backroom to pick it up. "Hello?" He was still going over paperwork and waiting for his nephew to get back from Nara. They had a lot to go over with new plans for their pack.

"Hey, um... I really need your help... I think I found my mate..." Sasume gets excited hearing from his nephew and learning that he has found his mate; however, he is not liking how worried Shirou's voice was sounding.

"What has happened? Tell me everything." Shirou interrupts his uncle "not now, no time, please just come to my home and see her, please."

Sasume nods his head then voices approvingly that he would come. "Yes, I'm coming, then I'll be there shortly then." After hanging up the phone, he grabs his medicine bag and heads out to his nephew's home at a brisk pace.

••Shirou••

I see my uncle come in the front door looking at me worriedly. "So please tell me why I'm here." He says urgently. Nodding my head, I pointed to the living room.

"I believe I had found my mate; the thing is she kind of passed out when she came to the threshold of my home." His eyebrows lifted as I said this. "So, let me see her; is she like us?"

My shoulders lift in a shrug. "To be honest, I'm not so sure; I sense that she isn't human that she is something more. I'm just not sure what. Oh, and she is not Japanese, she's American." At this, my uncle stops in his tracks and just looks back at me questionably.

"What!? How did you communicate with her? When did you learn English??" I shook my head at his questions. "No, no, she speaks Japanese there's no question that she was raised here..." I grabbed at him and drug him to the futon where she was still sleeping.

"So why is she here, Shirou? Where did she come from?" I waved that off, for now, wanting him to scrutinize her.

My uncle was slightly younger than me, so he could get carried away and was distracted easily; I wanted him to stay focused on her health. He was a very bright doctor for his age and was a sought after doctor, especially by his female patients who would fight over appointments just to be seen by him.

He looked at Mitsuki then back at me and had the nerve to smirk at me. "So, did you find this one on your last mission or what?" I shook my head. "No, you know I don't have time for such things. However, I did find her asleep on the Naito estate, at least right outside it, on my way back.

I guess I had been watching her all night. I wasn't quite sure if she was ok or not and really was afraid to scare her or bother her while she slept, so I chose to just watch over her 'til morning, especially when I caught her scent. I doubted until I had touched her and had been drawn to her, so I'm pretty positive that she is my mate.

She was acting strangely, though, and not showing that she felt the pull, so I'm not sure what could be wrong if anything?" Sasume looked at me and knelt beside her. "She's really attractive... I'm not even her mate and find her beautiful, especially for a western girl." I unconsciously growled when he said this. He continued talking, ignoring my slight outburst.

"I thought they would be a bit bigger in size? She is so tiny" he then took her hand on his checking her pulse; I found it puzzling that he jerked his hand back at first and had a strange look on his face for just a second; then, as nothing happened, he looked down at his watch and calculated the time to her pulse. "Seems to be too fast for a human's pulse, so she is definitely not human unless she is going through an attack." His voice seemed a bit strained but had his doctors face on.

Sasume than forced her eyes open one at a time, shining light in each eye, then removing the light; her eyes were like emeralds, deep green and shiny he was taken by their beauty. He was concerned that the whole time he was examining her that she had not awakened, he let out a frustrated sigh and shook his head, looking back at me.

"What is her name again?" I was looking at Mitsuki for a while then back down at him as he was still kneeling next to her. "Mitsu...Takeda Mitsuki." His eyes never left mine, and his eyes widened a bit. "Did you say, Takeda!? Oh... just great, how long did you say she was here?

Do you realize who that family is!? It just not possible! I really hope she is not the same young woman that had disappeared two years ago. If she is ... she has a lot of explaining to do when her family finds her. I seriously don't think you or I will want to be too close by when they do."

I grabbed Sasume's arm rather roughly. "I think we should let her decide what is to happen with her and her family, for right now, can you keep her a secret until we learn more... I mean, so we can see if she is in danger or something?

She seemed really stressed out, and then passing out like this, there must be a reason, and seeing as she is more than likely my mate and the future Luna, it's my responsibility to take care of her. So please keep this to yourself."

I let his arm go. I knelt and picked Mitsuki up in my arms and carried her to the guest room, laying her on the bed, and walked out, sliding the door shut slowly.

"I will protect her; I will watch over her, and we will try to find out if she is from the Koroshi-ya Okami no mure (Assassin Pack) or the Shuryo (the termination pack) you speak of, then maybe we can see or better yet, she can tell us what is going on and if someone is after her."

I didn't like thinking that she belonged to anyone but me, crazy I know, because I just met her, but I'll be damned that someone takes her away from me now that I just met her. This is the safest place for her, well for now anyway. Sasume just looked at me and shook his head.

"Well, I hope you know what you're getting yourself into... I must get going just let her sleep; she looks like she is just extremely exhausted. She must have been walking for several days without food; I promise not to mention her to anyone, for all of our sakes." He said the last few words in a near whisper, but I was still able to catch on to them.

I watched as he left my home and saw him glance up at the window where she is; he had a sad look like he didn't really want to go. I walked back to the kitchen now that it was already noon, I guess breakfast is out of the question.

Opening the fridge and took out some ingredients, and started cooking. I think Okayu (rice porridge) would be ok for her; it's not too heavy. Plus, I feel as though I could eat some too. Smiling back as I made my mom's recipe of Okayu, my sister and I loved the heck out of it when we were sick, and she'd make this for us.

─────────── Awake ───────────

It had been at least an hour had passed since my uncle had left, and I started hearing her move around in the bedroom. I put the food out on the dining table and left to go check on Mitsu.

As I opened the sliding door, I saw her stretch out on the bed; I sauntered over to the corner of the bed and sat on the far corner. I was only several centimeters away from her one of her feet. I looked at her foot and let my eyes traced up to her lovely slender legs that were exposed to her well-formed rear.

My cheeks were flaming with heat; my eyes darted away quickly, then back at her; I reached over to the hem of her dress, gently tugging at it, making the rest of her dress covered her legs that were exposed as I did. Her body was now more defined and showed more of her perfect figure.

I spent a few minutes admiring and marking into my memory the incredible view before me. Not able to stop me, I leaned over and gave a light, innocent kiss to her temple feeling the sparks of pleasure as I touched her.

I had to pull myself away from her, then standing up off the bed and went back downstairs to the kitchen. Grabbing some utensils then bringing them to the table, making sure everything was in order and in place.

I could hear her moving around again, but she had gotten off the bed. And now she was walking around the room. I didn't want her to panic, so I rushed upstairs again, opening the door and into the room.

I noticed that she was a little dazed and not looking like she remembered where she was; I hurried by her side and started to try and calm her down. I finally was able to get her to sit down as I rubbed her back; she began to relax. I started to explain who I was and where she was.

••Mitsuki••

Suddenly, I woke up in a strange bed and in a strange room. I sat up in a hurry, which was probably one of the worst ideas that I have conjured up so far. Grabbing my head as it felt like it was spinning out of control. I tried to remember where the heck I was; the room was relatively straightforward, had some scrolls hanging, some with text, and some were just paintings of animals and samurai.

As I stumbled trying to get my bearings, I see the door fly open, and a wonderful and familiar scent flooded my nose vetiver, musk, and hint citrus. I moaned softly to myself as the smell seemed to calm me a little swirling through my maze-like brain; I could think of nothing more calming.

I looked at the man standing there; he was tall, a firm looking broad shoulders, and dark hair that seemed to whip around his face loosely. His eyes were dark brown with flecks of gold hinting around his irises so piercing and profound. So handsome, he had to be the most handsome man I've ever seen.

Still lost in my thoughts, I didn't notice him get closer; he was saying something. All I could focus on was the sweet tone of his voice; it was terrific, and then he put his hand and the small of my back and started moving his hand in small circles, which felt very calming as well. This person was definitely a godsend to my nerves.

I could feel my cheeks steaming as he continued talking and touching my back. I heard him let out a small sigh as I looked up at him; his face had the sweetest expression on him that I covered my face quickly, not knowing how I was looking at that moment.

"No, really, it's fine you're only tired is all, was someone after you, where is it you are trying to get to, do you remember?" As he asked this, I took my hands away from my face seeing he was really concerned for me. I kept looking at him and shook my head no, as I started rubbing my head as to wipe away the pain I was still feeling.

"My head really hurts badly; I'm not sure what happened; how long has it been now?"

He smiles down at me, kindly gently moving a strand of hair out of my face and sliding it smoothly behind my ear. "Well, for at least three hours now. I was not really watching the clock, but my uncle Sasume came and saw you make sure it was nothing too serious.

He thought you were just really exhausted, and that is why you were in that condition." I showed no expression as he spoke; I wasn't sure if I remembered correctly or not, so I didn't want to say too much about my condition, plus

I need to know if he knows certain things and people first. I don't want to put myself in a more harmful situation than I already am.

He must earn my trust before I let too much out to him, but this connection I feel towards him is not working in my favor. Still grabbing the side of my head, I whimpered softly. The pain was increasing, running down the side of my face internally, killing me, going through my ears and throat that when I tried to swallow, it was impossible. I placed my fingers over my ear, applying pressure to it. When I did this, the pain wasn't as bad as it was.

I closed my eyes, and my body started to relax again and felt limp from the pain. I walked over to the bed and laid down again, letting out a soft sigh. I saw the man I now know as Shirou walk towards the bed and sitting right next to me, he slowly lifted my body up from behind my arms and pulled me closer to him like I was a small child laying me against his chest.

He was so warm and being so close to him, and he felt so right I did not fight him at all. He was practically a stranger, but he didn't feel like one at all, not knowing one thing about him but feeling as though I've known him my whole life. The comfort level was too high when he touched me.

So warm and firm. I felt my eyes close and

then felt as he started to lie down, bringing me closer to him, encircling his arms around me. My body was totally relaxed, feeling blissful as my cheek rested on his chest, feeling his chest rise and fall smoothly, smelling his scent, and feeling his warmth was indeed bliss.

I have never been comforted like this in my life, my mother sometimes had held me, but it was definitely a different feeling when I was sick growing up. My dad was hardly ever home, so she had never been held like this by the opposite sex.

I thought it was very nice. I had never dated, and I didn't really see myself as attractive by any means. I was small and petite and really have never caught anyone's attention before. So, anyone's affection was unexpected. I wasn't sure what to think as Shirou held me in his arms like this.

4

UNFORTUNATE EVENTS

(20 years ago)

••Takeda Nanami••

I'm so thrilled my husband Mitsuo has told me we will be staying in America for several years. It had been a wish of mine to travel abroad and learn new things and meet new people. I have been tied down too long in my father's pack and really wanted to leave.

I've always heard that there were more established packs in America, so I was delighted that Mitsuo allowed me to join him. He knew that I was depressed about not being able to get pregnant and that this would be a good distraction.

I had packed our bags, which were only a few since he told me not to take much that we could buy the things we needed there in America.

We gathered everything and said a small farewell to our family and friends as we headed out to the airport and then an eleven-hour flight to our destination.

We knew that we would have to make another conjoining flight to our final destination once we got to America, which was only about two hours to Seattle, Washington.

Someone from the Red Moon pack was assigned to meet us at the airport and take us back. We will be staying with them now for quite a while. The Beta Rick Sterling came up to us and guided us to his vehicle after pleasantries. He seems friendly and courteous he knew several languages, which helped us communicate, and I assumed that was why he was sent to meet with us.

My husband knew some Basic English but was very broken; I only knew greetings and to ask of the bathroom. I was quite embarrassed as I muddled through the greetings. The man spoke fast, and it was hard to catch until he switched back to Japanese, which he said very well. He talked to my husband as he drove out of the airport and through the city.

There were very tall trees, and it was so green everywhere. The weather was slightly overcast but pleasant since it was nearly 15°C. It was April, and for a change, no rain today. They said they were expecting it later in the week, though.

As we arrived at the packhouse, we left the car and walked up the drive. I wasn't really listening to what the Beta had to say was more caught up on the children who were running everywhere playing with each other this brought a smile to my face listening to their laughter and yelling as they ran past us; there were two older teens who were watching after them attentively in case of accidents.

They had such colorful hair, some golden, brown, black, and red too. It was nice to see such beautiful children running around. I love children, as you could have guessed. I always wanted to be a teacher of younger children than I wanted to be a mother, too, but that was unfortunate since I have been denied such blessings.

There was a young mother that was sitting on the porch with a tiny baby. The baby had reddish curls that were just cuddling the baby's head soft velvety curls. I walked closer to her with a smile; she noticed me walking towards her, and she smiled and tried to introduce herself.

I had difficulties understanding everything she was trying to say but the Beta filled in what I lacked to understand. Her name was Lacy Marie Black, and she just had twins not too long ago; apparently, she was holding one while the other was inside and wasn't allowed to be outside due to some weakness.

There must have been things lost in translation because it seemed as though she had given up on the other baby who was a girl saying it was weak and had no future. I was uncertain how a mother could decide that their children weren't worth an effort. I only smiled and asked her if I might be allowed to see the child.

She looked at me like I was crazy for a moment. I'm guessing it was because I was new and didn't know anyone, and here I was asking to see a baby of a stranger, a baby that she's deemed unworthy of attention. She spoke to the Beta, who I was told was her brother, and he then spoke to me, smiling and gladly showing me the way to the child.

My husband looked worried about the whole ordeal. He wasn't sure that I should be involved with this but knew that I loved children so much that he couldn't say no to me. I felt that he knew and understood more of what was going on, but I would have to ask him later.

As the Beta walked through the home, he brought us up to the third floor where we would be staying so we could drop off our things. It was a huge room and had a connecting bathroom that led into another room. Which he said we could use both rooms for whatever we might need them for. Later, he showed us back downstairs to the second floor, and down the hall, we came to a very small room that had a small window to the side of the wall.

There was a small brown crib that was set in the middle of the room, and around the room, there were shelves that held linen, towels, and sheets. As we walked into the room and looked inside the crib, there was a very tiny baby in a plain white onesie on bare white crib sheet bumper padding around the crib, which was also white.

The baby was beautiful; she had reddish curls like the other one we had seen in the front with its mother. This little one was so much smaller than her brother and her face with such pale skin, tiny little hands, and feet. I looked to the Beta to see if I could pick her up; he looked terrified but nodded at me hurriedly. I looked at him, puzzled but turned around and gently picked her up, supporting her head and neck doing so. She looked like a porcelain doll, a costly one.

As I picked her up, she opened her eyes, and they at first had a golden hue then changed into a deep emerald green color, which surprised me since she looked no more than a week old. She cooed sweetly as she looked at me, and the Beta let out a heavy breath as if he had been holding it in for a while. I ignored the Beta and brought her to my chest. I patted her softly on the back, gently rocking and humming to her.

"How long has it been since the baby has eaten?" "not sure," he replies. "Can you bring me bottled milk?" he replies again, "yes." So thankful that this man was fluent in Japanese, and also was pleased to know he would bring her milk. He must've mind linked one of his family because not too long, a young girl showed up with one shortly after.

I took the bottle and thanked the girl; the girl did a double-take as she saw me holding the baby and rushed out of the room quietly. I brought the bottle up to the baby's mouth after checking the temperature of the milk; it was lukewarm, so I gently massaged the baby's lips with the nipple, and she latched on and started drinking the milk.

It didn't take her long to finish the bottle of milk was about 266ml, a pretty impressive intake for such a small child.

••Lacy Marie Black••

((A few weeks earlier)) "Ahh, my water broke!!" I'm so scared, not knowing if these children will be alright; I have already been through a lot. I was taken away from my pack about four months ago by witches after being introduced as Luna of the Red Moon Pack. My new mate Jendrick Black who was Alpha, was murdered after he had marked and mated with me; it was also after we were officially announced as Alpha and Luna of the pack.

Jendrick was my childhood friend as well as my brothers, who was his best friend since they were children. He was only three years older than me, but I had shortly returned from college as I was away for four years, and when I returned, I was shocked to find my childhood friend was my destiny, my love, my mate.

News had spread fast of the Red Moon Alpha finding his mate, was so ironic that we had already known each other so well it made it so much easier for us when we found out. We couldn't stay separate for a moment; He claimed me only seconds after finding out, and I happily allowed it to happen; I let him mark me, and in between our high, I marked him hurriedly as well.

It was literally the happiest moment in my life, and it lasted a long and eventful night. No one in the pack was surprised at how fast we reciprocated our love and need for one another. There was no taking it slow; it was lustful and needing.

I had never been involved with any other I patiently waited for my mate, so there was no need to wait any longer, especially when I knew my mate so well anyway.

It was so unfortunate and devastating when our gathering of the Pack ceremony was interrupted by men and women alike, they were dressed in dark garbs chanting something, and arms were raised above their heads. It happened so fast that our response was not quick enough.

All I saw was Jendrick leap from the stage, and in midair, he transformed into his Wolf. So many wolves and witches fighting.

I then snapped at out of confusion; I started to gather the young and elderly pushing them through the Packhouse into a makeshift basement. I remembered these corridors when I was shoved through them once before when I was a child during many rouge attacks.

I worried about the warriors, my brother, who was now a Beta, and of course, I was apprehensive about my new mate, childhood friend, and lover.

Fighting against witches was tricky and very dangerous; they are unpredictable, always using new ways to attack, very cunning. I found them to be more so than the hunters who occasionally came through our lands and tried to take out a few of us, but this was too scary.

I can't stand things I don't understand, and

I don't understand the witches. I don't know their motives and needs; they are just too mysterious, and to me, that makes them dangerous.

After taking a batch of the pack, I turned back to find more that might not have found their way to the basement. I ran out of the door and to the opening when I was sharply hit from behind, rendering me unconscious.

I woke up in a darkened room; my eyes took a while to adjust; I noticed I was on a medical bed with a strange man looming over me. I struggled to get up but realized that my arms and legs were chained and bound, spreading me across the bed.

My clothing was torn, and the man who seemed like he was the one responsible for my current situation noticed I was awake. He held no expression at all; like a blank slate, he looked down at me with no emotion, which made me more afraid—not knowing exactly what he was planning to do.

He slowly brought his hands closer to my clothes and started to rip the rest of the shirt, opening it down to its hem. Then flipping the material, opening it to reveal my chest and stomach, he grabbed ahold of my skirt and yanked it, trying to rip its layers but was having difficulty doing so.

While he was doing this, I was yelling at him, trying to get his attention to stop. I was hoping he would show pity, remorse, anything. Nothing, he had no emotion for what he was doing; instead, the monstrous man walked away for a moment and brought a sharp pair of shears, which heightened my worries—not knowing if he was planning to stab me to death with them. I let out a high pitch screech, which surprisingly must have startled him because he finally snapped and then lashed out, slapping me.

He still didn't say anything, but now he had a hateful expression on his face. "Look, you son of a bitch let me go now!" He looked down at me directly with the scissors and started cutting off my skirt; he lifted the material so as not to cut or scratch my skin, then pulled the remainder of the skirt from my body and threw it to the floor.

My face was covered in tears as I was sobbing, wishing this was just a nightmare. I felt his rough hand against my stomach; it was big in size and rough calloused from whatever work he usually did. I squeezed my eyes shut and tried to escape from my own dilemma; I wanted just to disappear and not exist.

He grabbed at my panties, ripping them away, throwing them to the floor with the rest of my clothing. He still had an angry look on his face as he got on the bed straddling me looking at my body, I could feel his eyes moving down my body; it disgusted me.

He shifted on top of me slightly. I was afraid to see what he was doing; I kept my eyes shut as he then brought his hand on my sex.

Rubbing his rough, calloused fingers against me, I let out another sob. With his other hand, he grabbed my throat and pressed down. Confused, I opened my eyes, letting more tears escape as he then let go of my sex, holding his penis, rubbing and hardening himself in front of me. As I let out more whimpers, he pushed down more tightly on my throat, making me struggle for air. He then placed himself at my entrance and plunged into me roughly. He filled me of him and moved his other hand over my throat but allowed me to take in a few breaths before closing down on me again, moving his hips harshly against me and shortly releasing himself inside me.

He took one hand off me and slapped me so hard on the face making my bottom lip bleed. I could taste the coppery liquid as it dripped in my mouth. Getting off of me, he left me there naked on the bed as another person took his place.

Walking in the room as the other stepped out, he had several syringes filled with some dark liquid. Another person who came in was a woman.

I was guessing she was a witch from her garb she was wearing. She couldn't really see her face, but her voice was all telling. She was speaking another language, so I couldn't know what she was saying but seemed as though they were instructions because the man nodded and seemed to follow whatever was being said.

He placed his hand on my abdomen then carefully stuck the needle all the way in me. I let out a painful cry as I couldn't move to get away from them; he only shooshed me to settle down. I started to hyperventilate as he drew out the first syringe as it was now empty.

The next two needles were then meant for my veins as he then found veins again; following the witches' instructions, he put the liquid inside me; after this was done, they left the room, allowing the first man to re-enter the room.

I wasn't sure who really came in until he was at my bedside; he leaned over me, looking over my body, and nods to himself, leaving me so confused about what the hell was going on. Being raped and then poked with needles, I wasn't sure what the plan with these people was as they asked nothing of me didn't utter a word to me.

The man then sat near my head and placed his hand against my face making me face him as he leaned further towards me, placing his lips upon my own. My eyes widened to him doing this, and I tried pulling my head away. Still, it was in vain as he kept me in place and started kissing me forcefully, snaking his nasty tongue on my lips.

I would not open my mouth for him, so he slapped my ass as I gasped from the sharp pain; he won, snaking his tongue in my mouth, trying to make my tongue react with his own.

I was disgusted, nearly gagging in this kiss; he didn't care, sucking on my tongue as he climbed over me again, sticking his big finger in my sex, moving it about as if it would excite me.

I was so grossed out there would never be any sexual excitement from me. I refused any of it. He didn't seem to care, still kissing me forcefully now, taking his finger out and placing his cock back into me, and he kissed down my neck. He latched onto one of my breasts as he lifted my ass off of the bed and plunged deeply in me, squeezing my ass as he repeatedly plunged into me until his final release.

As his body relaxed above mine, he nipped my nipple hard and moved off of me. He smirked down at me as I turned my head with a disgusted look away from him, still tears flooding down my face.

He again stood and left the room, saying nothing to me. No one came in, for I'm not sure how long possibly ten to twelve hours. When someone did, they brought water and an apple and nothing more and didn't say anything to me either.

It was good because I wouldn't be talking to them either I just wanted to die. It must have been at least a week later when I finally heard voices excitedly from outside the door. Then when someone pushed open the doors, I saw my brother looking down at me, still naked and bound to the bed with urine stains below me as they never removed me from the ground to allow me to defecate in the appropriate place.

He had a scary face as he took off his shirt after getting the chains and latches off of my arms and legs; placing the shirt over my head to cover my body, he lifted me and ran me out of the building. He was furious but held me gently as they got into a car and took me back to the Packhouse. I am sure that my body looked frail, and that must have frightened him.

I could feel all the anger he had inside from the pack bond and also now could feel as though something was missing. That is when my world started to crumble. The cruel truth was in front of me when they informed me that the Alpha was dead as well as several of our best warriors.

I was just lucky enough to still have my brother with me. I was utterly broken, and they had to build me back up to function correctly. I was unfit to be a Luna in my current state, so other packs had joined with us after hearing of what happened to me and my Pack and my mate. They helped us so much, keeping the flow of things like order, training, and necessary protection of the Pack, as well as my recovery.

I left nothing out as I explained to my brother what had happened to me, although he never told me how they found me. I found out weeks later of my pregnancy, not sure if it was due to the rape or of my mate, I chose to keep the offspring. Days to weeks and weeks to months, my stomach grew, finding out that after four months, I was to have these children no going back now.

So, they rushed me into the room into a tub that was filled with warm water. I lowered myself into the water as the contractions were strong; the urge to push was great.

The first child, which was a boy to come out, was a pretty average size of 7lb 09oz, then bearing down again about ten minutes later, I delivered a little girl of 4lb. The boy was very normal looking, but the baby girl was something much more; her eyes should have been like her brothers but wasn't they had been gold in color, which frightened many, claiming it was the witches doing. I began to believe this too, not wanting to see her anymore, I sent her away.

5

QUIETLY LITTLE FOX

••Beta Rick Sterling••

I am happy that my sister is ok but devastated for what has happened to her as well as our pack. We have suffered losses that were senseless losses. I wish I was stronger and that our Alpha wasn't taken from us so quickly; he didn't even know that his mate was taken when he died.

The witches had done something terrible the way he died; I will never forget. It was like he had imploded; it was horrific. The only good thing was I don't think he felt anything, not like what my sister had gone through and felt.

When we caught up to her from one of our trackers, they had already left her tied to that damn bed. It made me sick to see her in such a state. I wanted to rip them to shreds, and I will when and if we find them, I will kill them slowly.

She had two babies yesterday, and I

wasn't sure if she would even look at the girl after she sent her away, saying that the baby was possessed from witchcraft. I wasn't so sure to me it seemed like a different type of changeling.

I've seen others from other places that have turned to bear or fox before, just not one born from a werewolf. It puzzled me as I tried to reassure and reason with my sister the possibilities. Those possibilities made her overly stressed, even more from the memory of what had happened to her when she was taken.

I left it alone feeling sorry for the child I had assigned someone to take care of her, but weird things kept happening to the caretakers, so they didn't last long. The baby would cause things to happen to them. One had lost their hearing from just picking her up. Just off the wall things being blamed on by the small baby.

Well, today, one of the visiting Alphas that had agreed to help out our pack while my sister and our Luna was still recovering. He had informed us that he had asked a friend of his to come in from a pack in Japan. Apparently, they were having some changes and recovery from their own pack and decided that it would be good for him to stay here while we needed the assistance, and they had business to deal with together anyway. My sister agreed hearing of Luna's predicament was slightly opposite of her own she thought maybe they could help each other out.

So, hearing of their arrival, I was waiting at the airport for them, patiently waiting for them to show with a sign with their name written in kanji. I was lucky that I had taken Japanese while in grade school and again in college, along with German and French, so I was quite helpful with international requests from the packs.

I lifted the sign a little more and then saw a Japanese couple walk towards me. I greeted them. The husband seemed to know quite a bit of English even so it was a bit broken as for his wife, it was very little, but I see that she tried her best. I explained what the situation was at the pack on the way back to the Packhouse. The Luna didn't seem to be listening much, but Alpha Takeda was very attentive to every word.

As we drove in the drive, he looked towards the house, and I heard a gasp from behind me. I smiled at the Luna in the review as she had the sweetest expression on her face as she watched the children playing in the yard.

I stopped the car, and she unsnapped herself and opened the door staring in awe of the many children who were so lively running about yelling back in forth to each other.

I saw her face almost drop as she saw our Luna, my sister, sitting on the rocker on the porch with Zachery, her baby boy.

She walked over rather gracefully, and as my sister tried her best to introduce herself. I had to step in and translate for the Luna, Kamishiro; she smiled and introduced herself as well; again, I translated into English back to my sister until she had asked to see my sister's other child.

At first, Lacy was reluctant to let her see her too soon she was afraid something might happen to the visiting Luna, but Luna Takeda had insisted on seeing the child she then said ok for me to guide her to her.

I'm sure Lacy didn't want them to run out of the pack from the child. She was very unpredictable on what she might do to any given person who would even go to the room.

I decided it would be best to let them put away their things; they didn't come here with much, which made me feel like they wouldn't stay long, and this is probably what my sister was thinking as well. The visiting couple followed me up to the 3rd floor.

I showed them the guest rooms that were to be used by them. There was a large Jack and Jill room with a bathroom in the middle that connected to the two rooms. They seemed surprised at the size of what was given to them for the time being. They smiled, and it seemed as though the visiting Luna wanted to see the baby now. I smiled and directed them to the second floor and down a hallway to where the small linen room was.

I opened the door revealing where the child was. I had a feeling that she would not like or agree to where we had kept her, but I had always made sure she was clean and always on clean bedding. My sister didn't want to know of her anymore and had abandoned her, and I felt sad for the tiny child as I felt it was not her fault how she came to be and of how small she was.

They both had their mother's hair; it was just that the girl's eyes were fiercer and had a fire behind them, which made my sister believe she was evil. I never thought such things, but I understood that she was definitely not the same as her brother and seemed that she would be powerful, given time.

I gave the nod to her as I watched as the Luna reached down and picked up the small child my breath caught in my throat as she lifted her to her chest; she watched as the baby looked up at her. I know she must have seen her eyes as her expression was changing in something like admiration and smiled down at the baby. I didn't realize I was holding in a breath 'til it escaped my lips. The Luna seemed like she was already in love with the child. She bounced the little baby lightly against her chest and hummed sweetly to her.

The Luna started questioning when her

feeding time was, and the last time she was fed, and for milk, I mind linked one of the caretakers for the bottle, and sure enough, Kathy rushes in with the bottle warm and ready for the baby.

She had been the only one who had continued to take care of her even though she wasn't entirely comfortable doing it, always careful not to upset the baby. The Luna thanked Kathy, who wasn't sure what was going on as she was surprised at the Luna's visit; she rushed out of the room as the Luna was checking the milk's temperature and then feeding her.

The Luna was delighted that the baby had finished her bottle smiling down at her; she asked me what her name was; I was lost for words as she didn't have one.

I explained the best I could to her husband and to her the situation but was afraid that some of what I was saying must not be coming out correctly or entirely right. I did mention that she was just being taken care of by individual pack members but not the mother.

She asked if she might be allowed to take care of her and possibly adopt her if no one had objections, her husband looked to me like he might have complaints himself but looked more afraid of his mate than the child and didn't say anything but if looks could speak words, they would be speaking volumes.

She ignored him and kept her eyes on me. I only nodded my head, knowing that my sister would not be the one to stop her from taking this child if she wanted it. She smiled up at me and looked at her husband, telling him that she wished for the crib to be moved to the room adjacent to theirs so that she could be closer to her.

He looked at me for the ok, and I smiled and said that would be perfect! I was just hoping that this arrangement would work out for all of us. I wanted the small baby to have a loving home, and with that Luna, I felt that would be possible.

##•Takeda Nanami••

It's been three weeks now, and the pack and their Luna Lacy Black had given me the ok to adopt her daughter as my own. I gave her an old family name that I thought suited her well, Takeda Mitsuki; her mousey features, she reminded me of my great aunt, who was part kitsune, especially her eyes, which held the same hue.

When I saw this, I seriously thought that this child was part Fox, no doubt in my mind I spoke to the Beta, and he also thought it might be possible since the unfortunate things that had happened to his sister the Luna. He said that his sister thinks she is a Majo, but I wasn't so sure of anything about them they held many mysteries of themselves, so there was no telling that this child could have the powers of what they call the witch.

I had no idea what spirit she would hold within herself either most of us only hold a wolf, but since I see fox traits, I wonder, could it be possible to hold both? We will see in years to come, for the fox do show themselves relatively young; however, the wolves take more time, usually when they are in their mid to late teens depending on their royalty status.

That is another thing I was interested in Mitsuki is that she showed signs of Kitsune with her eyes. This is so young to hold her color of the Fox. Bright gold, they would turn as she was upset for anything.

Two years have passed, and it is time for us to head back to Japan our home we have been away from our pack but have gained a grand Alliance with many of the American Packs.

My husband has helped the other Alphas find a vital placement for the Blood Moon pack Alpha, who has now joined with Luna Lacy her family name has changed to Willard instead of Black. The new Alpha Jeremey is very brave but sweet to the Luna, and their bond has grown tightly, which is essential for her pack. They will be strong together, which makes me happy for them.

I'm excited to get back home with our new family. Our pack can't wait to see their new member. Even though she is still so young, she has grown healthy, walking around and starting to talk, which is so cute.

Her long red curls fall passed her shoulders, and such green eyes sparkled when she giggles and plays. How much in love is my husband and myself with her? She has worked her way into Mitsuo's heart, and he won't let her out of his sight when we are out. When we arrived in Japan, we were so exhausted I can't believe how active this little girl has been thank goodness she wasn't crying and didn't through her fits, which can be very dangerous since her powers come out in the open.

Random things happening I haven't experienced anything too scary be have been told when not in my presence, she can be a little terror. Nope, this trip involved running around, talking, or babbling everyone's ears off, singing little tunes to us (loudly), and drawing, which I preferred to everything else she had in mind.

It was an exceptionally long trip. Let's just say it felt as though everyone on the plane was happy to get out and away from us when we finally landed. We definitely had our hands full with her.

Well, we were driven to our home and saw everyone greeting us happy we were back, and they couldn't keep their eyes off of Mitsuki, so I introduced her to them as they all wanted to play with her. I spoke to one of my Aunts who had kitsune in her lineage, and she agreed that she might just be a hybrid of kitsune and wolf, which was quite rare. Some she said don't make it passed the first year.

Mitsuki is now Ten years old, walking around without a care in the world. She gets along with everyone as if she was born here. She attends grade school and is very bright, catches on to everything she's been given, and is more studious.

They have placed her passed her expected grade level, and so she attends the Lower Secondary school or a Junior High level. They won't move her to the higher Secondary School until the age of twelve, but she seems to get bored now with her classes. So, we will probably be moving her out into a private High school so she can challenge herself appropriately.

Only a few days from now, she will be eleven years old, and she walks around so humbly and helps whoever she can. She still relatively high energy but still so very small, which is a challenge for her too since she is brilliant yet so very small.

Wow, it's the first day as a sophomore in High School. She is 12 years old now still hasn't grown much since she was ten it's driving her nuts, but we tell her she is so strong she has been studying many different forms of martial arts and weaponry classes and does exceptionally well.

She's starting to have bursts of fevers every so often, which has been bothering me. I've taken her to the pack doctors, and they said they usually see this in teens who are about to shift. I was arguing with them about how young she was, but they also reminded me that she might be Kitsune and if that is the case, she could shift anytime now, from age 12-16, which to me was such a large time gap.

Late at night, it happened she finally started her shifting process several weeks later from when we spoke to the doctors. I kept her surrounded by my sister and aunt since they said she might be flighty after the shift. Our job was to keep her calm; it would be difficult for us since none of us were Fox.

Not sure if our wolf would be able to link with her in her fox form. My aunt decided to transform prematurely and wait her out.

We sat with her as she was sweating profusely, and she started to feel the shift crying in pain; she doubled over, and her bones began to snap in and out of place, her body slowly taking shape into a small kit. Not quite a full-grown fox, orangish-red thick fur covered her body, eyes were golden and ear tips black with her hind and forequarters covered in short black fur.

She was a beautiful human child, but wow, absolutely a gorgeous little kit. We tried talking to her as she looked around wildly; the doctor wasn't kidding when he said they were very flighty. She looked as though she would run away as soon as she found an opening.

She let out a strange cry that sounded half like a howl was deafening. She did this multiple times and looked around and seemed to be waiting for an answer, but no answer came back to her.

My aunt started to try to talk with her. She only looked at her and made a scream again, which was such an eerie sound. My bones shook wildly as her voice rattled through them. My sister made a mistake of moving towards her and seeing an opening, and she darted passed both of us, moving so fast into the thicket.

We both shifted; the three of us followed after her. My husband, who heard us through the mind link, had rushed out on foot and also shifted, running into the forest in hopes of finding her.

I'm sure she was frightened, so we must find her and calm her down before she leaves our territory. No telling who she would run into off of our land so many rogues and spirits that would try and trick her.

I saw Mitsuo's wolf pass by us in a flash as he moved quickly through the briars; he looked as though he caught a glimpse of her as he then quickly changed direction. We followed him.

I called out to her, trying to mind-link to her in hopes that she could hear me. Then I stopped fast as I heard growling from ahead. I could tell it wasn't Mitsuo, so I tried moving away from it than seeing a brown, tawny wolf-headed straight for me. I had to leap at him to get a hold of him before he could get me than seeing my Aunt rush in grabbing at his throat as I pinned down his shoulder, she had successfully snapped his neck, we quickly left before more Rogues showed up.

Mitsuo mind-linked all three of us that he had Mitsuki, and he was bringing her back; he asked us to meet in the pack home. When I got to the house, I walked in, and quite the sight was the Alpha (Mitsuo) with a kit in his mouth. If I only had a camera, it was the cutest thing I've seen. I smirked at the sight of them. He looked as though he rolled his Wolf eyes at me.

Walking into another room, I shifted and got dressed, then came back to get her from him. She was squirming, but I held onto her as he left to shift and get dressed. He came back in his human form; as he did, she started screaming again, which almost made me drop her.

Freaking me out with such awful noises, I held to her 'til he closed us in the room, telling me to place her down. As I put her on the chair, she looked up at us, he spoke to her calmly. "Easy little fox, shift." She looked at him and yowled at him loudly.

"Quietly little fox, now shift," he said in a much more demanding Alpha tone. She quickly started to shift. He turned himself around as I placed a blanket around her body. She was back to herself, but it must have been too much as she fell asleep immediately after.

6

THE UNEXPECTED

••Takeda's••

Now graduating at the age of fourteen, and she has been fighting us tooth and nail to whether or not she would be able to handle college on her own; at such an age, most kids would be starting high school.

We were concerned about other things that we didn't talk about anymore, but the concern was still there. She spent time in a preparatory class at one of the local colleges to see if she could handle the curriculum. She did very well taking the exams to see what courses she would be able to take as well as which schools would be optional.

She was super delighted at the age of fifteen; she is now in college and doing so well, we as her parents, couldn't be more proud of her.

Four years later, we are at her graduation. Now at the age of nineteen, she has her life ahead of her, and she is ready for anything. Well, at least for her, she is coming home with us to see the pack since she first left us four years ago.

The pack is excited to see her, but she said she had no interest in staying too long and wanted to start placing applications into individual businesses as a business analyst. Who is responsible for improving a company's competitiveness and performance, striving to identify new ways to control costs, increase efficiency, or improve sales?

She had gone to college for this line of work knowing it would be beneficial for her father's business, halfway through she had lost interest in her family's business and want to expand to other regions.

She had also majored in many languages since it came quickly for her. She studied in English, German, French as well as the Spanish languages. We felt that she would have many more openings and diversity with this as a skill.

Mitsuki has come home, and it's been several days of her conversing with different members of the family; they all were wondering where and what she would be doing next. She was happy seeing everyone at the pack home. She was hardly around while in high school and even less while in College; she rarely came back on holiday, so we hadn't seen her for years.

Everything was right as it should be until nightfall when we got a disturbing notice. "If you don't turn over the girl, there will be consequences towards your whole pack. She is no worth to you anyway; someone will be waiting on the East Setouchi in-port arena.

Get her there tonight. Don't make a big fuss about this or else, oh, and we have your young pack member Shiro if you want, we can start with him."

On the bottom of the note, there was an embossed image of a crow or raven. The picture seemed to be inked in blood.

(2 years from present time)

••Mitsuki••

Everyone in the pack has been acting rather peculiar after I have arrived at the family's manor. I started getting strange vibes since I was twelve years old. After my birthday, all of them had been asking to be off the wall questions about fox and wolves. Since when was I an animal expert?

They also often wondered if I had remembered the night of my birthday, but I couldn't remember anything then suddenly, the questions just stopped as fast as they had started.

When I was finally going to high school, I was happier since it was a boarding school, and I would get something more familiar and not have to be looked at weirdly by my own family like they were expecting more out of me.

It seemed as though they thought something interesting was going to happen, and it freaked me out too much. I fought my parents a lot to even allow me to go to college; I kept saying I was ready, so I compromised by going into preparatory classes, which thankfully was counted as a duel credit, so I wasn't wasting my time with it.

Shortly after, they allowed me to enroll and attend classes, another blessing since the college wasn't nearby, which meant I got to board there, and I made up my mind to stay.

Not that I didn't love and appreciate my family, but I didn't want or need the distractions from them. I had a few friends in college but mainly kept to myself since I was so young.

I had no need for loud people around me; it made me nervous, and I have always been content with staying by myself, a very solitary creature.

Well, getting back to what was happening tonight, the family decided that it would be great to throw a get together to celebrate my graduation day. That's when things started getting weird one of my cousins had bumped into me, giving me a quick glance and darted off in the opposite direction with a paper and an odd-looking arrow.

I was really tempted to follow him to see what it was, but as I started walking in his direction, my aunt grabbed my arm and hauled me through the front door and towards her car with a forced smile. "Let's go for a ride?" She pondered.

She didn't sound convincing like she was being forced to go. I wasn't so inclined; I didn't feel like going anywhere, not when I just got back to the manor. It hadn't been even 30 minutes, and I was asked to go for a drive? I had been in the car long enough on the way home, so nope, not my idea of fun.

"I'm tired of being in a car, so it will have to wait; why don't you ask Akito to go with you? He was just running around anyway, and maybe you can ask why he looks so suspicious." I whined to her. She shook her head, looking nervously at me.

I turned my back to her and started to go back into the house and felt her grab my hand roughly, and she opened the car door and pushed me in. As she shut the door, I saw my uncle in the driver's seat. I was so surprised that I didn't have time to get out of the car.

My aunt got in the backseat, and my uncle started driving away. It had been a while since being back here, so I wasn't sure where we were going as I saw the docks, they stopped the car and told me to wait at the port. I turned around to my aunt and started to ask why, but she was afraid; the fear in her eyes as she shook her head at me and told me to get out, almost yelling at me.

This day was completely turned upside down, and I wasn't sure what to make of it. I opened the door of the car and stepped outside; it was already getting dark; it must have been close to six in the evening.

I looked back at her, and then my uncle leaned over and shut the door from the inside; he then pulled away from where I was standing, leaving me all alone at the port. I was so focused on the car pulling away from that I didn't see a woman was standing not too far from where I was. I first heard the clacking of shoes on the pavement and turned to see who was there.

"Who's there?" I asked in a weary voice. In the shadows, I see a woman strolling towards me; she started talking to me in English, which surprised me. "Is your name Mitsuki?" Her eyes were intense as she stared at me as if she would miss something if she were to look away. I just looked at her cautiously, not wanting to say much to this foreigner.

She got closer to me, and I could make out her golden hair that was mid-length and slightly wavy. She was wearing a dark cloak that reached down to her ankles. She gave off an eerie vibe as she got closer. I started to feel nauseous, my stomach doing flips as she spoke again. "Mitsuki comes to me now." she sang out to me. I hated this.

This woman seemed dangerous; everything about her was wrong. It was an illusion, and I feel as though she wasn't real. "You belong to us; you have no home here, come with me now." She said in a non-sincere voice.

As she moved towards me, she was no longer making any noises, no steps heard.

She was now gliding steadily towards me; this made the hairs on the back of my neck stand. I heard a high-pitched tone loudly in my ears and started to see nothing but white. I closed my eyes and held my head; something inside me told me to run and to do so quickly.

As I had heard this, my eyes flashed open; I took off dashing through the streets and into a near forest, running over roots and through low lying branches.

The bag I carried got caught a few times on the trees, but I yanked them free as I rushed through them. I don't know how long I was running must have been for a long while, but I felt winded and slowed down. I listened to anybody that might have followed me but heard nothing.

My anxiety must have caught up to me, though, because I started crying out of nowhere. Not sure why I was left at the port then being scared half to death by some strange woman that was waiting for me.

I started to wonder if my parents knew what was going on. For my aunt and uncle to just leave me out there was just too strange, what the hell??

Well, I am a grownup now and can't be depending too much on them now, but still. I couldn't believe what just happened; it made no sense to me at all. It's not like I wanted to go back to the manor, and it looks to me; some didn't want me to return. So be it! I was never the wild free type with no plans, but I guess I have no choice now.

It didn't feel like I was wanted at the Manor, so I think I will just walk to the nearest town, village, or city that might be nearby. It was late, so I decided just to pick a place to lie down and rest. I had maybe rested for an hour or two when my eyes flashed open, and again I had the urge to run away from where I was; I picked up my bags, and it was so very dark some light loomed down from the moonlight, and my eyes adjusted the best they could as I worked my way through the thicket of the forest—holding tightly to what I had left of myself, my identity. I was a mess. I wasn't sure where I was going; it felt as though something was pulling me along, though.

It must have been at least an hour that I had

been running off and on. In between, I would walk than have the urge to make a run for it. I was exhausted, so I stopped where I was and crumpled to the ground again, too tired to care, and fell asleep again. Waking up to the morning light and in the middle of the damn forest. The grass was damp, as were my clothes from the morning dew. I kept going through the forest and got excited when I start to see signs of civilization, a sign, and also pavement. "Oh, thank god, I'm out of the woods!!"

Seeing a mile marker to Nagano, I was relieved not really familiar with the area but very glad to be away from Ozumimachi. So, I had traveled an outrageous and unbelievable number of miles in one night. Not looking a gifted horse in the mouth, I didn't question it at all. I just kept moving, knowing that I had to get further away.

As I was walking, there were cars coming and going. I was hoping to meet someone going near to Fujisawa, so I walked to the SA (service area); it's the safest way to catch a private drive with someone without having to stop traffic, which I knew would capture the police's eye.

I didn't need that; I just thought of being in Fujisawa, there was a conglomerate business I was interested in pushing an app for anyway.

Even if I could get a temp position, it would

be the best thing for me to be able to prove myself! So, I arrived at the SA and was fortunate to run into a family they were from Tokyo and said they could get me to at least that far which I was more than happy with that!

They were surprised that I was actually a Japanese citizen when they saw me; they had taken me for a tourist. I laughed at this kindly and told them I was actually adopted but now on my way for business.

I didn't want to dump my issues on to them, so I kept it brief and simple. So, two and a half hours later, we arrived in Tokyo. I thanked the family; they were very sweet and thoughtful as they wished me good luck and a rich blessing to my future. I bowed graciously and walked away to find a hotel to stay in for a while. I needed to clean myself and needed some quality sleep in a bed.

In the next few weeks, I have been looking for an apartment as well as putting in applications to many financial companies in Tokyo and Fujisawa, I got a call to talk with a landlord, so my hopes are up.

I had been turned away previously because of my age and no proof of income, even though I have savings, so frustrating I am now thinking it would be best to have a roommate or something, nevermind that I can't stand to be living with strangers. Still, I could just treat it like I did in college.

I'm just happy I am finally getting closer to my career. I had a feeling that it wouldn't come easy for me being a young female, and also being Caucasian doesn't help here either, not mattering if I was raised here or not.

Nothing seemed likely, but with patience and with my credentials, it should work.

Please, god, let it work. The meeting with the landlord finally came, and again I was denied. So I decided to go the college route going to a university billboard and finding some requests for roommates (probably should have done this, to begin with).

I take a few slips of papers with the shared housing info and go back to the hotel. When I get there, I get out the papers and look at the requirements of what they want in a housemate, finding two that I felt would be best.

I gave them both a call one I had left a message with, and the other I heard a guy's voice answer. I spoke with the young man, and he agreed to meet up with me after he was done with his classes for the day; he said three other students lived there and that it was a coed home, with six bedrooms and that they were hoping to find two more residents to fill in the homemaking payments more doable.

That evening I freshened up and walked to

the shared house; luckily, it was within walking distance. I brought my credentials with me in my bag.

As I rang the doorbell, I looked around the outside of the home; an eye-catching statue of wolves was at the corner of the entrance. My fingers traced around the ears of one of the wolves; it was made of a smooth stone.

It was an eerie feeling when I looked into the eyes of the statue like I've peered into eyes like these before. The door opened, and the man stared at me before letting out a small cough to get my attention. I quickly looked over to him, yanking my hand away from the statue. A girl appeared behind him, and her eyes widened and swear "Okami" left her lips. The man nodded and murmured "Kitsune" too,

I wasn't sure why they were mentioning wolves and fox, but I stood patiently for them to let me in. That didn't seem like it was going to happen anytime soon. I was getting fed up quickly.

"So, uh is Shinzo here? I'm here for a room." They both had raised brows, then I heard the same voice from the earlier phone call and turned around to see the young man I was guessing to be Shinzo.

I introduced myself, and they all smiled kind of weirdly and then welcomed me in. I followed Shinzo in the home as he was just coming in from class late. "Sorry for not being here on time. I got held over a bit. I am truly impressed with your Japanese. I seriously thought you were from up north.

Where did you learn to speak?" This was utterly getting to be the norm for me as I grew up in Japan, and with a Japanese family, I had long ago adopted the language as well as the customs just like my family had adopted me.

I explained to them in short how I was raised and taken in during infancy, so I don't know any different. They all seemed too interested in me, and it started making me feel uncomfortable as it always did when I explained this part of my life to anyone.

Plus, for some reason, I let slip the fact of why I am here at all besides trying to find a job in the corporate world. They seemed to be in disbelief as I mentioned the women after me; I wasn't sure if I should have even mentioned her, but I let my guard down with them, and they seemed really interested.

They went ahead and invited me to stay for dinner since all of them were currently home than afterward, I would return to the hotel. I seem to have fit their needs, so I was welcomed to stay and was allowed to move in the next day.

When I come back tomorrow, I will be shown my room and be given a chore list, which would change every week on rotation with the rest of the housemates. It was getting late, so the young man decided that he would walk me back to the hotel.

He said his fair wells as I walked into my room, and I waved back and thanked him for the consideration of walking me home.

The following morning, I gathered all my things to be packed and ready to move to the newer group home. I called a taxi, so I wouldn't have to carry everything while I walk all the way back. I loaded up the cab and asked the hotel to forward anyone who had asked for me to the new house number, in hopes that a job offer would be coming through for me.

I arrived at the community house and let myself in. Now that I am a resident, I no longer need to knock. I unloaded my things from the taxi to my new room, not that I own many things.

I haven't purchased much since I moved here to Tokyo. Just sets of clothing books and journals, nothing more. All set up in my room, I head downstairs to go out to get lunch. It's been relatively quiet and easy-going in the neighborhood despite it being so close to the University.

7

THE GETAWAY

••Mitsuki••

Regular days have come and gone; it's been a year since I came to Tokyo, but today, I feel it would be different. That's when I get a notice, I have been here for ten months now in the share house, and the message has come from an unexpected source...my mom.

I don't know how she found me, but if she could locate me so quickly in a big city like Tokyo, I'm afraid anyone could. I used the shared home phone and called back to find out why she was interested in talking with me since my aunt and uncle pretty much gave me over to a weird person that looked to do me harm.

"Hello, is Nanami there?" I wasn't sure if I should be even calling her at all. The voice on the other end seemed strained, but I could then hear them yell out for her as I heard them place the earpiece down.

"Hello? She answered I answered,

"Hi mom, it's me, Mitsuki," hearing a gasp from her than her reply.

"Mitsuki, is it really you?" I let out a sigh hearing her voice, still contemplating whether or not I should even be talking to her. I thought I was free from her 'til I received that makeshift letter.

"How did you find me, mother? I thought the family had wanted me gone since Aunt and Uncle abandoned me to some stranger." I said tiredly.

"What!? I was told you left on your own..." She said, sounding concerned.

"No, now you know I wasn't, someone had been chasing me though I believe that they don't know where I am now, and I really would like it to stay like that.

They seemed to want to hurt me. I have really bad feelings about them." I tried to explain.

"You are wise to no end, my child, stay away from people who you don't know. Don't trust anyone; I will not try to find you anymore; if you promise to stay safe and contact me frequently, you will probably have to move from where you are there are people who are looking for you still. They are not good people, Mitsuki. They are evil and will want to use you."

She wasn't making sense to me; I was so confused about what she was saying.

"Who are they, and why do they want me?" I asked. "They are witches." She said bluntly. "What!?" Witches aren't real, right!?

You're kidding... I heard someone shift their body weight behind me as they spoke,

"Oh no, they are real!"

It was Shinzo; he had a hateful look on his face as he said so. I heard my mom start to yell and ask who was here with me, but I cut her off.

"Look, mom, I'm going to go," then hung the phone up as I turned to face Shinzo questionably. "Why are you involved with witches?" He asked.

I looked at him dubiously. Not sure how to reply to him. I asked him if he was a witch.

"Absolutely not," he stated sharply. I nodded my head and sighed in relief.

"Well, my mother said they wanted me for something?" He looked at me like he wanted to say or ask me something like it was killing him.

I rolled my eyes. "What?? What do you want to ask me? I can see it in your eyes that you have something to say."

"Yes, well, I have many things that are bothering me now that you brought up witches. Like why your mother would have to warn you of witches? Or why you haven't shifted."

He started interrogating me. "Shifted?" What do you mean shifted?" His eyes widened unbelievably,

"Well, you smell like fox and wolf, so it's confusing. I figured at; first, it was because you might have hung out with friends who are but then I noticed you don't go anywhere and don't really mingle with others."

He said, stepping closer to me and leaned over, smelling at my neck. I know I must have gotten at least five shades darker as I was getting hot with his closeness. I pressed my hands against his chest to push him away.

"You're too close!" I warned.

"And you have the most interesting scent. I can smell the fox but also wolf with something else too. Very interesting and confusing. This might be why these witches are after you, you know? You might not be safe here. I'm only an Omega; I am not strong enough to help you by myself. "

An Omega? My parents also talked a lot about the Greek letters so weird." He looked at me, genuinely shocked after I said that.

"There must be a reason they didn't want you to know. What was your father? Was he a Beta?" He asked curiously. "They referred to him as an Alpha." Again, his eyes widened. "Then it is not my place to say anything more.

He must have his reasons, and it's not my place to interfere as you are not my mate." He said, not thinking. "Your mate??" I asked. "Oh, ah nothing, not worry about that, uh sorry."

He blushes and turns away from me as if running away. "I've probably said way too much as it is." He said as he rushed to his room and shut his door with and slam.

I flinched at the sound, shrugging my shoulders, and walked out of the home.

I had to go to the library to return some materials. As I reached the library's entrance, I had started to feel eyes upon me as I walked in. I looked around, seeing many tables that were in the middle of a room and shelves stacked high to the ceiling filled with books.

The tables were filled with a mixture of school students as well as adults with papers and some with laptops opened along with books for essays and research materials.

I walked to the librarian returning some books and other materials that I had previously checked out, smiled, and said my farewells, and left the library.

Walking to the cafe that was at least two blocks away, I still had a feeling that someone was watching me as I was walking, ignoring this feeling, I reached the Cafe and stepped inside, hearing the little bell ding as I open and shut the door. I sat at a table by the window so I could watch people walking along the sidewalk.

As a waiter asked me what I would like, a few more people came to the cafe. "Earl Grey Black, please," I asked the waiter.

He nodded and went back to the counter. I figure it would do me some good to shake the stress I was feeling with my mom and roommate acting so peculiar.

Again, I get the feeling of someone's stares; my eyes flit around the cafe; it's somewhat filled with customers now. Not noticing anyone suspicious, I lowered my head on my hands, my elbows propping them up from the table. I push my hair, smoothing it out, and breathe slowly out.

The waiter returns with my tea thanking him, then picking up the cup to sip at the tea quietly. I look up and catch several people that must have just recently walked in looking at me and talking to each other the hairs on the back of my neck freakin' rose as I get a sickening feeling at the same time.

I lazily take out what I owe and leave it on the table and nearly stagger out of the cafe. I felt weak suddenly and continued to keep walking, frequently glancing behind me.

A man who walked around one of the buildings as I was passing him grabbed my arm quickly.

"Come with me, little fox"

I looked up at him with a gasp as he wrapped his arm around the back of my waist, as I was being led and then shoved into a blue sedan.

He slid in the car next to me in the backseat. "Don't worry, we are friends of Shinzo; we will have to get you out of town. We have been following you as asked by Shinzo, and we aren't the only ones following you.

You are not safe here; you need to leave Tokyo now." I looked at him and nodded my head.

"Is this about the witches? Did they find me?" "Hmm... yes they are a problem, foreign ones at that.

I'm guessing they came from your homeland?" I shrug my shoulders. "I don't know where they are from or why they follow me." "Well, whoever they are, it's not good or safe for you." He sighed, seemingly annoyed now. "We will take you to the Shinkansen. I suggest you take it to the Kawaguchiko Station and travel south near Shizuoka. There is a family that can help you there.

Don't take the train to Shizuoka though some have reported native witch activity in Shizuoka city limits, so stay clear of the city stay in the wooded areas when traveling from Fuji to Shizuoka."

He handed me a pouch filled with money. "This is from Shinzo and his housemates. He asked me to give it to you to replace some of your funds from the down payment of living. He also said to stay in touch, so when you get to a safe location, they can send you your belongings."

He then smiled at me as we arrived next to the station. "Take care and stay vigilant little fox." I smiled back and nodded at him as I waved goodbye getting out my travel card and swiping it, going into the terminal.

I turned back as I saw them drive away. He was charming. I hope I get to see them again.

I'm also not sure why I adopted such a name from him, but I was sure it had to do with what Shinzo had mentioned to me earlier. A fox smell, huh?

I Sniff my clothes as I walked through the opening of the train. Do I really have the scent of a fox? What do they smell like anyway, and how the heck would he know what they even smell like!?

Ugh, whatever. It just brings back memories from my childhood when I was continuously being asked by my parents about a fox and wolves, and something about feeling changes or something like that was so weird and got annoying too—another reason I wanted to leave. I'm totally not much of a social creature. I stay to myself, and I'm very much sufficient when no one notices me or talks to me.

The train trip was fast, snickering to myself at the thought ... just what you can expect for a bullet train. I liked it; I didn't have to spend a long time with people all around me. Especially the men and women who loved to spray strong perfumes and colognes on them; I have always been too sensitive to the pungent smells like that.

I always preferred the earthy aromas vs. artificial fragrances, which always gave me headaches in the end. When we arrived at Kawaguchiko station, I jumped up from my seat and got out of the train rather quickly and walked out towards the maps in the station.

I had to find my way to Shizuoka, and what was a fun idea is I would do this by taxi and on foot. I hail a cab that was close to the station, and we set for the city of Minobu.

As we arrived, I asked to be dropped off at a local hotel and paid the Taxi driver. I went to a small hotel and was able to get a room. I tried my best to remain quiet and unseen as not to attract any attention from anyone.

Waking in the room and sliding the door shut to the room, I take out a tatami mat and lay down. Curling up into a ball, I finally fall asleep. The next morning, I get out of the room and pay the hotel receptionists turning the key in and leave.

I decided to pack up some food for hiking, seeing as though I would not be taking too many transports and be walking a lot. So, I stopped in a few local shops buying some change of clothes as well as shoes that would last and a map of the local area. Not sure how that would go, I thought I would give it a try. Then to a grocery and purchasing nonperishables to last a few days at most.

I started heading further south to Onuta, hoping to stay not too far from the roads and stay mostly in the woods as instructed. I felt if I stayed somewhat near the road, I wouldn't get too lost in the forests.

Few hours had passed, and I have been

getting tired, every now and then, I hear strange noises, but I'm starting to get used to the noises of the forest. I sometimes see wisps floating above the ground ever since I was a child; I have always believed them to be some form of yokai or yurei.

I always felt and said to others if you were really quiet around them, you could hear their voices. I laid down on my jacket over the lush grass and watched the wisps dance in the distance as my eyes start to get heavy and close.

My eyes open with the rising of the sun, I slowly sit up and stretch out my arms and legs, letting out a small yawn. My arm is sore from laying on it all night, and I'm sure I have impressions of twigs and rocks on my arms. I let out a groan and stand. I look around some trees for a safe place to do my business, then come back to my bag, taking out hand sanitizer and cleaning my hands before touching some of the rations. I eat some food and take several sips out of the canteen. Then putting the remains back in the bag and start walking again.

A week of the same view until reaching Shiozawa, then took a taxi to Nishigaya. I stayed in a hotel just for a bath and finding that I was close to Shizuoka, which made me leave the same day and not worry about staying at the hotel amongst too many people who might be looking for me.

I stopped in the local grocery and picked up more food, protein bars, and water. Didn't take me long 'til I was on my way again further south, walking in the woods of Shizuoka.

"Well, it's been three days, three days, and nothing to show for it. Now I am furthest from everything then I have ever been before." I say again to the open air.

Looking around, I spotted a small group of bushes and took off my coat, laying it down over the bushes, kneeling down onto the coat laying my head on to the coat looking upward, not seeing anything only hearing the small nightingales bounce around in the trees singing melodies as it grew later and later in the night. My eyes began to close slowly, and I was fast asleep.

8

CLOSER IN A DAY

(current day)

••Mitsuki••

I woke up with Shirou's arm around my waist, holding me; I looked up at him; he looked like a model so masculine and has very handsome features. I could feel his firm chest and abs pressed against me, and he smelt heavenly.

He was so warm, too; I'm still surprised at myself. I really thought without a doubt that I was asexual; I never dated anyone and had no interest in men or women.

There was something about Shirou that pulled me towards him and made me feel safe and not wanting to run from him as I have with others in the past. As I pulled myself from my thoughts, I realized that he was now awake and looking down at me, smiling. I quickly looked down from the embarrassment of being caught staring at him. He placed his hand under my chin, pressing upward to meet my gaze again.

"Please don't look away from me. I love the

way the light hits your eyes. So beautiful, like shining emeralds." He said softly. I knew my face had to be burning red like a furnace; I was so embarrassed. "Oh, uh, it's just that I've never been so close to anyone, and I still just barely met you."

I stammered. He nodded, understanding my predicament, then sat up in the bed, releasing me for a moment until he was comfortable and then sat me up against him. "I'm sorry, but I can't seem to let you go yet. You see, it's hard for me to explain to you, but I have been looking for you everywhere."

I nearly became unnerved by his comment, thinking he might be a witch, I started to panic.

"Uh, are you... Uhm... are you a Majo? He looked at me alarmingly and then shook his head.

"No, I'm not; they are bad news around this area. Why do you think so??" He asked briskly.

"Well, I was told to come to Shizuoka for safety from the witches. I came here from Tokyo...hmm, for about two weeks now?" I said nervously.

"Oh, who sent you to Shizuoka?" As he asked me this, I turned around sitting opposite him as I was trying to think of what I should be telling him. "Well, when I was in Tokyo, I found out that witches were following me and that they had been looking for me for a long time. When a man, a friend of Shinzo, my housemate had told me it was no longer safe and took me to the train station, I then was told to get off before arriving at Shizuoka and walk the rest of the way in the path of the woods, as to avoid witches along the way."

He quietly listened to me as I spoke, not questioning or interrupting me, as I explained. When I was clearly done talking, he looked back up at me and paused for a moment as if he was thinking about something, then like a light switch was turned out in his head, his expression had changed. "It must have been the Shiroi Tsuki pack.

What did he look like the man who helped you?" I looked at him like he was nuts. I don't have a great memory when it comes to random people, mostly when it was someone that I've met for just a short time.

I scratched my head with my hand and thought hard. It took me a while, but I tried my best to think of him. "Well, I guess he was around 177cm tall, he had mid-length dark brown hair that wasn't quite touching his shoulders. He had a slight go-tee that was more stubbled than long, lightest brown eyes, a stern brow but a pleasant voice? Maybe 64kg? I really am not sure; he kind of surprised me and grabbed me, pushing me into a car with him. So, it happened so fast...sorry." As I said the last bit, I swear I heard a growl, but his facial expression remained the same. "Sounds like Takeuchi-san, a warrior from the Shiroi Pack."

"Pack?" I asked curiously. "My family has also slipped the word Pack as described before. Shinzo also said things of packs and Greek alphabets too.

Can you please explain things to me?" His brow raised as he rubbed his chin, looking at me as if he had things to say but not knowing how to go about it. I was good at reading people, and this was definitely the issue he was expressing at the moment.

He had the same expression as Shinzo when he had things to say but felt conflicted because of my father and something to do with an Alpha status.

"Please, just tell me, I can see you know something, won't you just tell me now that I've shared too?"

I gave a pleading look towards him. It must have been my doey eyes that got him; he sighed and nodded his head.

"Ok, little Fox, I'll tell you." My eyes looked fiercely at him and his choice of words.

"Why did you call me that? You aren't the only one who has called me this either."

He looked somewhat regretful as he started to talk to me and explained what he could.

"Well, that's what you are uh... well, at least

that's part of who you are anyway? You have a strong fox scent along with a wolf too, and something else is blended, but I'm not sure what it is, to be honest. But your fox scent is overpowering when you are upset. Well, I can try to explain somethings to you, but I'm not sure if I should say everything at once. Do you know of changelings? Kitsune, werewolves, and werebears?"

"Hmm, I guess so? But like witches, I thought of them as myths. I guess if there are magical things like Majo, Wisps, Yokai, and Yurei, than there would be room for werewolves, kitsune too."

He chuckled at my response.

"So, you believe in yurei and yokai?" "Yes, well, I do see them on occasion," I answered.

"Oh, I see. Well, yes, so getting back to the werewolves and kitsune. I believe you to be either both or at least a kitsune. You have a strong aura about you too. Have you never shifted into a fox?" I lowered my head, remembering all the times I was questioned by my mom and dad when I was twelve, that horrible birthday that I can barely even recall. Shirou saw that the subject was bothering me.

"Can you share what you are feeling with me? I want to help you understand what you don't. I think if you share with me that you can overcome what is upsetting you right now."

"Well, ok. When I was twelve, something devastating must have happened. I, unfortunately, don't even remember what had happened, but ever since my birthday, they, oh uh, my parents had been asking over and over about that evening. Kept bringing up fox and wolves and asking if I'd seen them in the forest by our home that night. Then all of a sudden, they quit asking. Like it never happened at all. I don't remember much, but when I sleep, I see a white wolf and a red fox, and sometimes they talk to me in my dreams."

As I looked up, I see him smiling so brightly at me. I wasn't sure what I was supposed to do or think. Was this a good thing? He gently took my hands in his and kissed them lightly while looking down at me.

"I can't wait any longer. May I ask what you feel when I hold your hands like this?" My breath caught in my throat; I looked down at our hands that were joined together. Slowly letting a breath out and then looking into his brown eyes, I answer him. "I feel very warm and nervous, but relaxed at the same time if that makes any sense at all."

I nervously say. "I also feel the power from you and a strong pull like feeling that draws me to you, making me want to stay near you. I've never felt like this towards anyone at all.

I've never liked to be this close to anyone before. I've always enjoyed being by myself and don't like talking to very many people at all." He nodded his head as he understood.

"I believe that the need for isolation or independence is your fox in you. They generally are solitary and not crazy social. I want to ask if you ever heard of Mono no unmei no ai or a mate?"

I think back to when Shinzo was mentioning a mate or at least me not being his.

"Well, sort of. I wasn't sure what Shinzo meant by me not being his mate." I heard another growl and looked up at Shirou. "Did you just growl?" He looked at me, targeted flushed, and started stammering. "Uh... well, I uh... damn it yes I uh...suppose I did."

My eyes rolled in my head, as it just dawned on me that he might be a wolf if he is doing that. "Are you a werewolf?" He smiled warmly at me and nodded his head rather proudly. "Oh, so you can change into a wolf then?"I asked him, somewhat surprised at this new situation. I was getting excited to see this transformation hoping he would show me.

He nodded then smiled, saying so. "Yes, I can shift into a wolf; however, I was hoping to discuss the mate pairing first. I truly believe that you are mine. You are my Mono no unmei no ai. My destined love, my mate."

He then pulled my hands towards him abruptly, making me fall into his chest than wrapping his arms around my waist. It happened so quickly it caught me off guard.

His face leaned into my neck as he took in a breath through his nose, smelling my scent off of my neck. As he slowly breathes out, his breath blows my neck softly and makes me shiver. "How can you tell? What do you feel when I am touching you?" As I ask, I leaned my face on his chest, letting my arms wrap around his back, pulling him into me.

He spoke into my neck as he continued to hold me comfortably. "When I first met you in the forest, I was drawn in by your scent.

I couldn't help myself, and when I saw you sleeping there, I wanted to do all I could to protect you. Still, in my wolf form, I had nuzzled you, and I felt a sharp spark on my face; it wasn't painful but rather pleasurable.

I knew then that you were definitely something very special to me, but I was worried and still am about your wolfs' presence or lack of. You see, normally, we can at least let our wolves communicate, but for some reason, my wolf, he can't talk to yours like she is hidden or missing."

He sounded unfortunate when he told me this. I felt his facelift, and he kissed my temple softly. "I would like you to meet my Uncle. He is our packs doctor, and I believe that he might be able to think of something.

He's brilliant, and plus, he has already met you once while you were passed out. Will you agree to meet him?"

I backed my head away from his body and looked at him. "Yes, I suppose that would be the best thing to do, and I feel like I can talk with him if you are here. Is he also a wolf?"

He looked really relieved at my answer and nodded his head. "Yes, this whole pack area is filled with wolves; there isn't anything else around for miles.

I'll mind link him and have him come over; he doesn't live too far from me since he lives in the main house."

We came down from the bedroom and waited in the living room sitting on the futon. We heard a knock at the front door, and Shirou called out, saying for him to come in. When the door opened, I was surprised to see a young man walking in. I suppose I was expecting an older gentleman once he had mentioned an uncle.

He was nice looking I'm sure other women would be falling at their feet for him had they seen him. He looked similar to Shirou but not as broad-shouldered and muscular as him. As he walked in, he smiled and started talking right away.

"So, I see sleeping beauty has finally awoken." He said in a cheery tone.

Shirou instinctively stood in front of me, wiping his hand on his face and sighing. "Don't say weird things, and please don't test me. We have been talking, and I believe she has her wolf as well as a fox within. She just hasn't been able to shift, and I was hoping you could help with that?" Shirou said in an exasperated tone. The uncle looked dubiously at Shirou.

"Have you shifted for her? I think if she sees your wolf, she will feel more of the pull, which might allow her to shift." He said to Shirou.

He walked around Shirou and came closer to me.

How old are you, and have you shifted before? He asked in interest. "I have just turned 20 last month, and I am not optimistic about whether or not I have ever shifted. I only see them in my dreams, a fox, and a wolf.

His eyes widened when I said this, and I merely shrugged my shoulders, facing him, not really looking at anything.

Shirou turned to face us both. "No, you know I just met her yesterday, right? Why, the hell would I want to scare my mate like that?" He said with an irritated tone and a scowl on his face. "Well, at any rate, I will ask her first." He said, rolling his eyes.

"Do you want to see my wolf, or are you not ready? He can be pushy for affection, so I just want to warn you." He said kindly. I looked at him first then nodded my head.

"I trust you; I can't say why really when I just met you, but I've felt like I have known you for a long time," I say confusingly. He smiled at me, nodding, and walks out of the room.

"It's the mating bond that makes you feel that way." His uncle explains.

"He will shift in the other room to not startle you, so don't worry, he's coming back."

I step a little towards the door wanting him to be back already. I felt strange without him near me; it was so weird to me.

Moments later, I see a large beautiful silver wolf with black glinting through his coat; he has large golden eyes. He walked towards me as I placed my hand out to him, his face pressed against my hand.

You know when you drag your feet across the carpet on a dry day, and when you touch someone and get a spark?

That is what it felt like when my hand touched the side of his wolf's muzzle; it was a fantastic feeling now I can almost experience what he was trying to explain to me. His wolf rubs his body against me as he walks around me, and his uncle told me to sit on the floor. I did so.

His wolf continued to rub his body against me as I pet his fur softly.

He rubbed his muzzle and head against the crook of my neck then began licking my face, ears, and neck and sitting next to me than laying down, placing his head in my lap. I continued to pet him softly around his ears and jowls.

I moved my hands down his neck and shoulders. I swear I could hear him make a chirp like sound as I continued to pet him. As he laid there enjoying my petting him, my body became hot and achy; his wolf whined and looked at me, sensing the change that started to happen within me.

As I continued, I get warmer and warmer. I was getting very uncomfortable. I gently stood up and tried to back away from his uncle and his wolf. The wolf also stood up and started to follow me, not letting me leave the room. He then faced his uncle, and the uncle nodded and walked out of the room.

I dashed upstairs, falling missing a few steps, but the wolf blocked me from falling, keeping me upright as I rushed into the bedroom. I felt sharp pains erupt all over my legs and arms.

I began to feel like my head was splitting in two, letting out a scream as I laid on the floor, his wolf stood over my body in a guarding posture.

All I could feel was direct pain enveloping my entire body. I heard myself let out a curdling howl as I shut my eyes tightly seemed like hours before I had no pain, and I slowly opened my eyes. I could still see his wolf over my body, but now I wasn't me; I was now an animal too.

I looked at my forepaws and could see white fur covering them. The wolf looked down at me, and I could now understand him. Kaori is his name; he is definitely strong and proud but seemingly eager to please me. He leaned down and licked my face almost nonstop until I tried to get up. He helped me by nudging my side with his head and helping me up on all fours. It was a fantastic feeling. I could feel my ears twitching on my head, and my tail slowly wagging back and forth.

Looking around, it seemed as though everything was more transparent now. I could hear through my thoughts and feelings that he was asking how I was; he was very concerned for me as well as my quick shift.

I started to slowly walk around, getting used to walking on all fours, walking around the room and pushed at the door.

"I want to go outside now, is it ok to do this?" I looked at Kaori.

"Yes, that would be great to run, but how about telling me your name?" He sounded amused in my head as he pressed his muzzle against my neck. "Mizuki is my name.

9

MIZUKI: BEAUTIFUL MOON

••Mizuki••

As I told him my name, I gleefully rush by him and down the stairs trying not to stumble with my new stance on four legs. When I got down the stairs,

I looked back to see if he was behind me, making him nearly run into me as he was chasing me. My tail was flicking back and forth as his body rubbed up against mine, making me chirp a little from his touch. He guided me to the back door for us to get out; it had a different lever and was easier to manage in our wolf form.

As we left the house, there were some onlookers from his pack still in human form; he looked at them as they slightly bowed their heads and were looking at me curiously since I was new. I ran into the thicket happily, experiencing new feelings, and happy to be out finally.

As I was running, Kaori was running beside me, nipping playfully at me, yips from both of us probably was heard throughout the forest as we ran. After spending time with my mate playing around and running, we ran up to a creak and laid down next to each other, and my head lowered on my forepaws as he laid his across my shoulders. I fell asleep like this feeling he gave me; I could feel his strength and love for me, which put me at peace.

As we returned to the packhouse, Kaori asked me why I hadn't shown myself to Mitsuki before now. I explained to him that I had been in contact within her while she slept, and many times I tried contacting her while she was awake but seemed nearly impossible since the kitsune Inari was leery of anyone finding out about us.

Kaori's perked straight up on his head when he heard of the fox. Is there a way I can meet her? I scoffed at this, thinking it was a waste of time dealing with such a flighty fox. I turned my head to him and let out a puff of air from my mouth. "You will be held accountable if Inari decides to flee from you.

She has done it once before. She becomes very unpredictable when she is even with me; she doesn't listen very well, so that's why we've not shown ourselves even to Mitsuki in fear that neither one of us would have enough control over her so that she doesn't get us killed." He looked at me pleadingly.

"Come on, and I don't think she will be able to deny our bond." I look at him dubiously.

"You know it's possible that she might have another mate other than you, right?" He growled angrily at that. "I will never allow that; all three of you belong to me!"

"hmmph.... this is on you be prepared, Alpha, she might not be in shape but don't underestimate her; she will be fast." I closed my eyes and released myself to Inari's control.

I could feel the anxiousness within her and hoped that she would genuinely keep us safe and not get us killed. I really hated giving her the control even if she is older than me.

••Inari••

I can't believe that Mizuki actually agreed to provide me with power; as I open my eyes and see silver and black wolf, I can feel a connection to, but my fear is overwhelming. My ears lowered against my head as I dropped myself to the ground crouching, my tailed tucked in between my legs as I look up at the wolf in front of me.

He whines at me, showing a head and body, making himself look much smaller than he actually is. Lying on his side and beckoning me to him. My head tilts to the side, cautiously, moving slowly towards him.

As I smell him, my tail still tucked and ears even lowered, I'm only centimeters from him, his golden eyes watching my every move; my head pops up as I hear something rushing towards us. My eyes widened, and my head turned towards the sound. Within seconds I dash away from everything heading into the woods.

••Kaori••

I watched as my beautiful mate is resting. I nuzzled my head in her white fur, taking in her scent; I felt so relaxed like nothing else in my life even matters. After a while, we start to head back; I got the dumbest idea in my head to see the fox.

I've never seen a kitsune before, and knowing that she too was my mate, I really felt the need to get to know her. I was clearly warned by Mizuki that it was a horrible idea, and she said that she would be unpredictable and a flight risk.

I really thought our bond would be strong enough to keep her near me and under control, and boy was I wrong. When she shifted into the kitsune, it was really magical and fantastic. She was just as gorgeous as her wolf form and as her human form.

I was struck dumb, seeing her as a kitsune, her beautiful coat was red with a white tuff at the end of her tail. She had four black legs and black tips on her tiny ears. She was so small and adorable; I really fought hard with myself to stay calm.

I lowered myself to the ground. I could sense her fear. I tried making myself as small as possible to not spook her into fleeing from me.

As she started to relax and come towards me, a numbskull wolf came to report to me, talk about lousy timing; all of a sudden, I see her ears prick upon her head, and she jumped and quickly scurried away. I was so pissed at Chuichi for bothering us and scaring her.

I growled viscously at him, and he stopped in his tracks and fell to the floor. His ears pressed down on his head as he was apologizing to me. I told him to return to the pack while I ran off, trying to find my mate. I had a feeling it wouldn't be comfortable while she was a kitsune.

I rushed through the trees weaving in and out, trying to mind-link her. I manage linked some of the guard warriors that were patrolling to let me know if they saw a red kitsune; they were confused but didn't argue.

I got a notice from the northwest bank, and so I ran quickly to that area, looking around nervously. I caught a glimpse of red fur as she ran past, and I took off again after her. It must have been a few yards before I caught up with her and cut her off.

I quickly, without thinking, reached for her and grabbed at her catching her by the scruff. She was so small that I was able to carry her back to the house. Still not having success in mind linking with her, I grew annoyed, not sure if I was being ignored or not.

I carried her all the way back and went through the backdoor mind linking my Uncle to come to the house. He was already there, and in his human form, he looked down at me with raised brows seeing the little kitsune in my mouth.

I didn't have to inform him of who it was. He walked over and carefully took Inari from me, trying not to let her go again and trying his best not to get bit by her.

••Shirou••

I rushed upstairs and shifted, plus putting on my clothes before rushing back downstairs to take Inari from Sasume. He had her wrapped in a blanket to keep from being scratched and bitten by her; it made it easier for me to take her from him. I slowly started to unwrap her from the blanket and softly petted her, nearly getting my hand snapped off by her.

I hear Sasume laughing his ass off at this, which made me mad, and out of anger, I yelled at him to leave in my Alpha tone, so he looked at me unhurt and unbothered by me and went back out the back door, securing it as he left.

I took my wrapped-up mate upstairs; when stepping into the guest room, I closed the door behind me. "There your fine no one will hurt you. Can you calm down now?" I looked at her and continued to talk to her in a calming voice, hoping that she would settle down.

She was so beautiful; her eyes were just something else. "Can you relax and let Mizuki or Mitsuki come out now?" I continued to pet her and started to feel her relax in my arms. I knelt down on the floor with her and sat down, just looking at her sweetly.

She looked back at me, and I relaxed my hold. She calmly stood up and walked off my lap, flicking her tail, she turned around and licked my arm that was already heeling from her bite from earlier. She looked sorry; I was hoping that I would be able to talk with her one day soon.

I really would love to know what she thinks of everything and of me. She sat and whimpered as she began to let herself shift back. I saw Mizuki, a stunning white wolf.

With the same color of eyes, a glittering gold hue so much brighter than my own. Mizuki looked over at me and was wagging her tail back and forth in such a happy motion I smiled at her goofily and raised my hand to pet her.

She rushed towards me, knocking me down and licking my face; laughing, I look at her sweetly, thinking how fortunate I am.

"You're so beautiful, Mizuki, all three of you are so very beautiful." She stopped wiggling everywhere and settled herself down, licking me again, then laid down, resting her head in my lap. I ran my hands gently down on her head and neck. I could feel a knot on her neck from where Kaori had a bit at her in her other form. I'm guessing that she is still healing from it.

"I'm sorry about that" she lifted her head and tilted it, not sure what I meant or why I was apologizing.

"This right here, does it hurt?" I could hear her purring voice in my head as she was trying to communicate; I could finally listen to her.

"No, I do not blame you, that was Kaori's decision, and I am just glad one of you could calm Inari; I was afraid for all three of us because she has never trusted anyone. I am glad she could work with you.

Even though she bit you, I'm so happy you are a patient, one Shirou. I am tired and afraid I'm not much company though I know Mitsuki will be no better when she arises; please continue to be patient with us as we get used to everything this is very new to us all."

She said as she then stood on all fours and walked back to me, licking me once again then turned away, once more hearing the crackling sounds of the shift, I see Mitsuki laying in a heap, her breathing was heavy.

I got up in a hurry and was kneeling over her picking up her naked body.

She was so exhausted, and it showed in her lovely yet tired face. I carried her to her bed and moved the sheets over her after laying her down on them. I turned to leave, but she quickly had my wrist in her hand. Turning back, I look at her sweetly. "Please don't leave me. Can you stay?" She said tiredly. I nodded my head and climbed in the bed next to her, laying myself beside her. She moved in closer to me, laying her head on my chest; I must be the happiest man on earth right now. I slid my arm underneath and around her back, placing a light kiss on her temple as her body is relaxed, she closed her eyes and fell asleep.

••Mitsuki••

I woke up in Shirou's arms; my body felt heavy and hard to move from all of the shiftings that had happened hours before. It must really take a toll on the body from three different species, this was my first time doing that, so I wasn't sure if it ever got any more comfortable.

While I was sleeping, I could see Mizuki and Inari they were arguing about something I can't remember now that I'm awake what it was about, though.

Feeling his warmth was super comforting and seemed like it was healing me as well. I didn't even realize that I was naked until I tried to move, making Shirou move as well, and when he did, he moved his body even closer to me and ended up grabbing my rear and pulling me over him. I let out a gasp a the feeling of being captured by him; I realize it wasn't his fault we were like this as I had asked him to stay without thinking of my own predicament of no clothes.

Plus, he is such a gentleman for not even taking the upper hand while I was sleeping; I must be a horrible person because I do want to do things to him. Since after the shift, my feelings have grown as well as my arousal for him, and let me say being in this position right now did not make it any easier, or maybe too easy?

His hands then slid against my skin from my rear to my back, making my body react to him outing a small moan like a purr, my traitorous vocal cords letting out such a sound. Shirou's eyes must have opened after my outburst as he smiled down at me and wrapped his other arm around me. It felt like a mixture of Hanabi and heaven as the sparks go through my body; it was euphoric.

My hands were now trapped against his chest, and his around my back. I slid my hands up a little to his shoulders and lifted myself up a little now, looking down at him.

"Can I kiss you?" He asked me this; my face must now be on fire. I slowly nodded my head shyly and leaned down closer to him, brushing my lips on his such a small and light kiss; his eyes looked at me hungrily, his hands moving up and passed my shoulders soothingly, over my neck, then softly through my hair he pulled my head closer to him and kissed me again with a little more force I moaned as I kissed him back moving my lips and slid my tongue against his bottom lip as he opened his mouth I slid my tongue inside his mouth I could feel his arousal below me through his pants as I now am straddling him his kisses grew more and more intense. I can feel him tug slightly at my hair as he changes the angles of his kisses, then slowly kissing my cheeks, jaw, and my neck; I was feeling so many intense feelings.

As he continued to kiss me, cupping my breast in his hands softly, he licked around the areola and suckled softly. Twirling his tongue around my nipple and nipping at the tip, I let out a groan; he moved over to the other doing the same before kissing down the valley of my breasts.

He placed both hands around me and rolled us, switching positions him now, straddling me and looking down at me. This was perfect. I could see his finely sculpted body over me. I've seen nothing else more alluring in my life. I could tell in his eyes the way he looked at me that he felt the same about me.

"How do you see me as now; do you recognize me as your mate? Will you accept me, and no other? I know we have just met, but I would really like to know what you are thinking right now." He asked in a careful tone.

His eyes were pleading me for an answer as he gently wiped a curl from my face with his palm. "Mizuki and I definitely agree that you are out mate; however, Inari still is unsure and timid of the whole situation. I, however, am not and do accept you and no other." I am not that social with others, and it will take time to get used to talking more with them more comfortably. But as you saw earlier, Inari is quite the flight risk and needs to find common ground with you and the others."

He looked at me, understanding what my point was, nodding his head and looking down at me lovingly.

"I don't want to rush things any more than they might be right now but your thoughts on the actual claiming?" I looked at him, not sure what he meant at all. "And how is it done? Is it not done through marriage? He smirked down at me.

"Well, that is one of the steps, but with us wolves, it is important to actually mark our mates to deter others from taking them for their own".

"Mark them, how is this done, and does it hurt?" Again, I see a small smile on his face;

he seems happy that I am actually interested enough to ask.

"Well, it is done usually during mating or, uh sex, I guess lessens the pain and builds up the pleasure the pair feel as they make their claim on each other. As for how it is done well, it's our wolves that take over while we are making love, and they both leave a bite mark on each other, which ends up leaving each other's scent on the other."

His face had grown shades of red during the explanations, which I'm sure I was flushed too, but I felt he was simply adorable as he explained himself very well.

"Oh, I see. So, it's nothing too hard then." He shakes his head.

"No, not hard, but I really want approval from all three of you. Before we even consider going any further. I felt relieved after he said that knowing that Inari might not be up to it right away."

10

KNOWING ONESELF

••Mitsuki••

I always thought that you have to honestly know and accept yourself before you can ever hope to understand and fully accept another. That's part of my problem, I'm sure, not really understanding the spirits within. I get three times the job with Inari, Mizuki as well as Mitsuki.

All three of us have such vast personalities—an unsure human with a compassionate wolf, with an independent and unsociable fox.

Boy, don't I feel like the luckiest girl (please note sarcasm). I do; however, I do truly feel lucky to be paired with such a mate and man as Shirou and wolf as Kaori.

They have been nothing short of a blessing, so patient and understanding with us. After our talk on mates, I had gone to the guest bathhouse and freshened up, and got dressed.

I had been stewing over our conversation while in the bath; there were only a few pack members that were also in the bathhouse. I'm guessing they were told to give me a bit of space before I went in because all I received were curious looks and brief smiles as they scurried away from where I walked into.

The men's' and women's' baths were

separated by a wall in the guest bathhouse. A mural filled the wall in the sento (which uses regular water while onsen uses natural hot spring water).

I was told they had an onsen not too far away and that it was enjoyable and relaxing to go to. Walking in the female's entrance, I head to the locker/changing room and strip down, grabbing my shampoo, conditioner, and towel than walking into the bathing room; it was beautiful, it had a large mural of a pack of wolves near a waterfall that ran into the river scene.

Stepping into the washing station, I sit on the stool and run the shower over myself and began to wash my skin and hair.

After I rinse myself free of soaps and debris, I then walk into the soaking area so that I can relax overworked muscles from shifting so often. The water is really hot, at least 40c in temperature.

As I walk into the water, I can feel the heat right away; I probably shouldn't have showered in cooler water as my body will have to adjust to the change now. I end up getting out sooner than planned but feel it was long enough. Grabbing my towel as I get out, I wrap myself up and walk to the changing room again, getting dressed and walking back to Shirou's home.

Walking into his home, I can smell shrimp;

walking into the kitchen, seeing tempura set out, made my mouth waters fiercely. Shirou looked at me, smiling.

"Please have a seat at the table; I'll bring the food out to you in a bit. I hope you don't mind, but I would like to introduce you to some more of my family. I would like you to meet Giana. She is my sister; she's pretty full of herself but is a good person.I would love for you to meet my brother too, but he is away with my dad at the moment, and I'm not sure when they are coming back."

As usual, it was a lot to take in, but I nod my head and go sit down like he had asked as I think over what he had said—hoping that I wouldn't come across rude to his sister.

I was trying to picture how she looked and act. I had already met his uncle, and he was nice like Shirou, so I was thinking that she might, well, hoping she will be the same.

He came in and out of the kitchen, placing rice and tempura out with daikon and soba noodles.

There was a knock on the door, and a high-pitched squeal is all I hear before getting glomped and nearly sent out of my chair. I damn near went into panic mode as I was not expecting that.

He looked at me, surprised as well, then looked very apologetic; he raised his voice to get her attention. "Giana! You can't just attack someone like that, especially not my mate!!" She looked down at her victim, smiling like a crazy person, but she really looked similar to her brother, just really pretty.

"Hi, I'm Shirou's sister Giana. I'm so happy that Shirou found his mate, and it's interesting that you are uh... how do I say this without being to forward, uh American?"

At first, I took it like a punch in the gut but could tell by the look on her face she meant no malice in what she said.

"Well, I am a Japanese citizen; my adoptive parents are Japanese and brought me back from America," I said more defensively then I meant to.

She looked rather apologetic then hugged me. "I can tell you have been brought up well. Who are your Parents?" She asked curiously.

"Takeda, my mother Nanami, and my father, Mitsuo." She looked at me shockingly in disbelief, "The Gokudo!? So, you are the one they are looking for?!"

Even Shirou looked at me, surprised by his sister's outburst.

I was confused as to why my family was in association with Gokudo. I knew it was like she was saying they were the damn Yakuza.

"Uhm., no, no, no, I don't think you have the right people, my family is not like that," I said in denial.

"I don't think she knows, not sure how that's even possible though how can you live with someone that long and not realize who they are?"

Looking at Shirou like he might reject me any moment, I start shaking my head. "No, I was barely thereafter, I started school. I was gone for at least eight years from high school and then the University, I haven't been home.

I don't remember many details before while in middle school. I was only 12 when I started High school and was 15 when I started college, so please believe me."

Giana's eyes nearly popped out of her head. "A tensai! What other surprises do you have for us?!?" Shirou's brow lifted. "I never asked, but how old are you?"

I smiled a little at his question. "I'm twenty years old, well about to be anyway."

My age was never really a concern for me; it was merely a number, so I didn't mind telling him. He nodded his head and tilted his head towards the table at the food.

"We better get to eating, or it's going to go to waste." I looked at him with relief and smiled. I was truly hungry. I hadn't had a big meal since I came here. Giana seemed happy to eat too; I repositioned my chair at their table. Shirou and Giana sat on either end of me, happily starting to serve me on a plate and continued to talk about regular and non-intrusive things.

After we had finished our meal, I helped pick up the plates and serving dishes, taking them to the kitchen.

As I sat the plates down, I feel Shirou's hand glide across my back around my waist and pull me into him; he looks at me, smiling down, drawing me into him as he kisses my cheek and runs small kisses across my cheek to my nose.

Slipping down to my lips, then pulling away, looking at me lovingly.

"I will protect you; no one will take you away from me. I hope that you understand that Kaori and I will never let you go to anyone."

I wrapped my arms around him and leaned into him closer, feeling his arms tighten around me securely. Giana bursts through the door and smiles at her brother and me.

"So, this is where you two were hiding? It's fine; I can take a hint; I'll show myself out. I hope to spend time with you, Mitsuki!" I nodded.

"I think that might be fun; see you tomorrow then?" I asked. She nodded and turned away, walking out with a wave and closing the front door as she left.

Taking me by the hand, we walk to the living area sitting on a very comfy couch. "I'm so glad summer is almost over; it will be nice to be able to cuddle with you when it gets cooler." He said softly, gently kissing my head. Looking at the TV, he grabs the remote and turns it on, Detective Kogoro Akechi VAMPIRE the drama seems to be on. Being tired, I rest my head against him and close my eyes; while he watches his show, I drift off asleep.

••Shirou••

If some ever told me there would be a time that I would be relaxed on the couch with my love in my arms watching my favorite show, I'd think you would be lying.

This is the most fantastic thing I've ever felt, Mitsuki, so close to me, and my inner self is in bliss.

I still can't believe that my mate is from one of the strongest families in Northern Japan.

When Giana put the information together, I almost didn't believe it myself, but for her to not even know what she was a part of really surprised me.

I'm not sure how they were able to keep her from finding out; all this information came in a hurry to her; however, it's all coming together now.

I remember that the Takeda's Alpha and Luna left Japan and stayed away for at least two years. No one from their pack let it slip to where they went or why they left. The place they left to is solved, just don't know why but I knew they had brought her back with them. I wasn't old enough back then to know or care when they had left and come back. I do remember it being a big ordeal in the Pack community to know where the head of the Koroshi-ya Okami no mure (the Assassin Pack) had gone; well, that's no mystery now.

I grimaced to myself thinking back to when my uncle had questioned about her family; he won't be too thrilled to know she is part of the family he fears most.

Mitsuki's head slipped off my shoulder. I didn't even notice she was asleep until her head started to fall in my lap.

I gently shifted my hips so that she could be more comfortable and ran my hands through her red curls. She is just so beautiful.

Through a mind link, "I'm here," Natsu, the Beta, was asking me where I was, cursing to myself because I hadn't told many about my mate.

Only my sister and uncle know Mitsuki's true identity, and I was worried that others would give me grief because of where she was from. Not only her family here in Japan but her also being a foreigner too.

I answered Natsu back, letting him know I

was at the house. I then quickly tried to reach out to Giana, "Hey, can you talk to Natsu please and update him gently on the current situation?"

I figured she wouldn't mind; it's her best friend anyway. "You sure, do you want him to know everything?" She asked me.

"Yes, please update him. I don't want him to feel like he was blindsided. Also, we need to talk to Oji-chan (grandfather) too. Sasume already knows; he has met her as well; Natsu and Oji-chan really are the only ones other than dad and Akifumi."

"All right, then I'll go and meet with Natsu and Oji-chan."

She seemed pleased to be the informant. As I was done with that, my arms rested over Mitsuki's back protectively, I will not let anyone or anything hurt her.

I must have fallen asleep on the couch when I had awoken; I was lying down facing Mitsuki, having her against the back of the couch. It must be morning now seeing sun rays beam through the windows.

She's cuddled up so close to me, and it feels so nice; I have to keep myself in check to not try anything more with her.

I run my fingers through her hair softly and lightly kiss her forehead as I get up and head to the bathroom upstairs; I hope that she doesn't wake while I'm gone.

Running the shower 'til it's hot than close the door behind me, stepping into the shower. After cleansing off my body, I turn off the water and step out, grabbing the towel and wiping off the access water.

Walking into the room with the towel wrapped around my waist, I grab some shorts out of my dresser and snatch a folded shirt that was set on top of the dresser and put it on and head downstairs to the kitchen.

I asked Giana to come by this morning, and I hope she is already here. As I open the door, she launches and grabs me in a tight hug.

"God, Giana, you really need to stop doing that!!" She looked at me, disappointingly.

"Oh, it's only you, where is Mitsuki?" She asked as she let me go disappointingly.

"Sleeping, I wanted your help making some delicious breakfast, though." Smiling knowingly, she nods and starts making preparations for breakfast.

We cooked up some sweet omelets with fruit on the side.

Giana was always the best omelet maker in our family, so I was hoping to impress my mate with delicious breakfast, and maybe she and Giana could bond more by going out and having a girl's day out type of thing.

••Mitsuki••

I suddenly am in a forest. I hear sounds of wild birds and other wildlife as I'm walking through the low lying trees, my fingers brush against them until I see a white wolf.

I'm more than positive that it is my wolf Mizuki as she moves closer to me and gently rubs her body against mine. It is such an odd feeling; there is a pain but no pain.

Her golden eyes stare into my soul as I start to hear her talk to me.
"There are many things that our family has kept from us. You need to trust our mate; he wants to help us, but both you and Inari need to TRUST!"
Her overbearing voice boomed through my body as she seemed to be scolding me. In the corner of my eye, I see Inari also cowering to Mizuki.
I didn't even notice her from the beginning, but that is how she was even with me. She was standoffish, which made it hard for us to properly bond with one another.

"Our two families, both have rejected us twice now! How can we trust this mate, and his family won't do the same? Once they learn of the hassles, the witches will cause!!"

Inari says with venom. "He said he would always protect us, right? I want to believe him, I really do.

I'm tired of running, and I want a family!" I say to both of them, although it was mainly directed at Inari. "How can you be so sure that he will betray us Inari, aren't you tired of being alone?"

"I know you enjoy your peace and quiet, but don't you ever get lonely and want someone else to love?" Mizuki also says to Inari.

We were trying not to gang up on her, but she had to see it from our perspective, for a change. We are all sitting next to each other within touching distance. I run my hand over Inari's red fur.

At first, she glared at me then thought better of it. I mean, we are all a part of each other. "We can't be at ends with each other. We really need to agree on what to do.

Suddenly a silver and black wolf walk towards us. We can feel the intensity of his presence. It was Kaori, Shirou's wolf. The three of us turned to look at him all at once.

"I will protect all three of you, with my very essence of being. No harm will come to you; I love you with all my heart and will use my strength and power to stop anyone."

He continued walking up towards us, rubbing up against my body, similar to how Mizuki had done. Still, his touch brought nothing but a pleasure to me, as it did for Mizuki and Inari, rubbing up against them as well and licking Inari on the head as he passed by her and sat next to me, looking into my eyes directly through my soul as if he could see everything.

He was so beautiful yet powerful. "Come here, little fox."

Surprisingly Inari complied and stood in front of him and me. He then turned to me and quickly tipped his head back towards her.

My eyes scrunched together at first, and then I nodded my head thinking I knew what he might want me to do.

I leaned over and softly picked her up in my arms. The power she was emitting was terrific, or so I thought it was coming just from her. Still, instead, it was as if we were polar opposites of power both so very different than they were pushing away and making it feel so very different.

"What do you feel, Inari?" He asked her while she was still in my arms.

She looked rather perplexed as she was thinking it over than looking straight into my eyes, she answered quite frankly. "Like a witch?" My eyes bulged as she said this, and my head shook crazily back in forth in denial. "No, there is no way this is true!"

I started crying, thinking that everyone would reject me. Maybe this is why no one wanted me, to begin with, was because I was holding the witch gene, but besides the witch, I was also wolf and fox.

"How is this even possible?" I cried out in fear.

"Not all witches are bad, you know. Since you were never taught by any of them, you can make your own decisions on what type of person to be. That is probably what kept Mizuki and Inari from being able to come out as they should have, though. You must know and accept who you truly are first, then everyone else will naturally feel comfortable around you. You will be able to trust others when they know they can trust you and who you are." Kaori said with understanding.

11

MATE

••Mitsuki••

I started to feel cold as I was still holding onto Inari. Then first it happened with Inari, her body began to fade as she licked my face, then she was gone.

Then I start to see Mizuki fade away as well, leaving me to look at Kaori. He nuzzled up to me, and then he began to fade as well.

"Don't worry, my mate Shirou and I will always be here for you. We both adore you so very much; we will never reject you. He said before he ultimately left me.

I was standing on my own and growing colder. All of a sudden, I could start to smell food. In a small moment, my eyes fluttered open and shut to adjust to the light in the room.

Shirou was no longer beside me on the couch, but I could hear voices coming from the kitchen. I slowly sat up, rubbing at my arms to warm them, then slowly start to walk in the dining area.

I quietly peeked into the kitchen, seeing a much-hyped Giana and a playful Shirou cooking and talking to one another. I hope one day I will be like that too, I thought to myself.

I turned my head around, then walked steadily up the stairs and into the guest restroom, washing up and getting myself dressed. I definitely have to get some more clothes. I'm on my last shirt and pair of shorts. I came down the stairs feeling refreshed. I round the corner and stub my toe into a counter.

Tears welled up as I sucked in a quick breath, trying to refrain from screaming in pain. Hopping on my other foot while grabbing at my injured toe, I plop down on the ground to see the damage.

There was a small cut, so nothing too serious just hurt like a dickens. I sat there for a moment, collecting and calming myself down, then stood up again and walked to the kitchen with tears still in my eyes.

"What happened?!" Is what I hear from Shirou as he saw my face still showing evidence of pain. He rushed over and looked over me, head to toe to see what had happened, and then saw the cut on my toe along with a purplish hue starting to form.

I was embarrassed and looking down, trying not to laugh and cry at the same time as my klutziness.

"I stubbed and cut my toe on your cabinet in the hall," I say in total embarrassment. Giana smirked at me.

"Don't feel bad. I've been telling him to move that for a while, and I keep catching my dang elbow on the corner of it." She said in a half-irritated, pointing to the top corner in an amused voice. "See how it's not just me, who plays victim to your strange house arrangements!" She says to Shirou wagging her finger playfully at him.

"Yes, ok, I know now."He says, raising his hands up defensively. Now leaning down and taking a closer look at my foot, that was throbbing still. I looked over at Giana, who now sported a knowing look over at me than at Shirou. "Aren't we going to eat breakfast?"

My eyes glistened at the mentioning of food. I smiled embarrassed at Shirou and placed my hand on his shoulder.

"I'm fine; it's just a small cut that will heal in no time! So, let's eat breakfast now!" I said excitedly.

He looked up at me and nodded. "That's fine, then please sit in this chair."

He said as he pulled out the same seat I sat in yesterday. They both went back into the kitchen and came out with omelets on breakfast plates.

My stomach growled when I saw the food being brought in. Just as I thought they didn't hear it, I got a smirk from them both as they walked to the table, setting down the plates. After the table was prepped with food and drinks, the two sat down at the table. Shirou sat really close to me, seemed more intimate than yesterday.

"I hope you like omelets, and I had Giana come over to make these thinking you might like them. As we were about to dig into the food, the door swung open, and Shirou and Giana's uncle Sasume had come in the back door.

It had happened rather quickly and caught me off guard when I felt a small shock of a kiss on my cheek, then seeing him move quickly around to Giana, hugging her. My eyes had shot open really wide, feeling a strong pull. I then heard Shirou growling at him. Giana was stifling a laugh, trying her best to hold it in. "Oh, you're feeling brave today, Oji-san."

She said in a playful voice, hitting him on the arm.

"Ahh, I think I still have a chance with her, don't you think? I mean, she's not even marked," he whispers to Gianna, with a devilish sneer. I'm not so sure he didn't want his nephew not to hear him as he didn't say it that quietly.

I see Shirou's body shaking and hear his rumbling growl as I lightly place my hand on his back; his body stiffened up at my touch, then he began to relax as I moved my fingers on his back in small circles.

"She is MY MATE. You are never to touch her like that EVER again!" He said to

Sasume in an overly stern voice. Giana just had an, I can't believe this, or I don't think you just did that look on her face towards Sasume. Sasume still had a look like he won some challenge on his face.

"So, you are joining us, Sasume?" He looks at me innocently as he nodded his head and sat next to Giana, facing Shirou and me. I placed my hand on Shirou's leg, and he flinched at first but relaxed even more so at my gentle touch.

Looking towards me, smiling so sweetly, and I smiled back at him. "Thank you for breakfast. I know you and Giana must have put a lot of effort into it."

I could see his face flush with embarrassment but still has a small smile as he continued to look at me. He dug into the omelets and started eating. I think just to get out of making more discussion on anything.

We all followed suit and also started eating the fluffy and sweet omelets. After breakfast, it seemed that Shirou was glued to my side. He didn't leave me for a hot minute.

I think due to Sasume's attitude toward me, not being marked had something to do with it. I started to feel extremely hot and uncomfortable and fidgety in the middle of the day.

While Shirou and Sasume were talking, I was talking to Giana. We were about to leave the house, but I started to feel worse, very feverish and lethargic.

Again, I feel an intense headache and begin to hear voices in my head. Let me say it's never a good thing for anyone to hear voices in their heads, and I'm not talking about mind links, which were not the same as this. Mind links are invasive but don't usually give you migraines like this. I feel as though I'm having a psychotic meltdown.

Grabbing at my head, I fall to the ground. Giana tries to grab my arms to keep me from falling to harshly, she yells at her brothers, and they both run in seeing me on the ground. Shirou lifts me up, and he takes me to his room and lays me down on the bed.

"She's having another episode." I heard Shirou say to them. All I can do is grab at my head, and whimpers are the only audible thing coming out of my mouth. Shirou climbed next to me in the bed and wrapped his arms around me, whispering comforting thoughts. Laying sweet kisses softly on my face in between the soft kisses, he whispers my name.

••Shirou••

As I see Sasume getting close to my fallen mate, I can feel Kaori coming unglued. He was losing his mind, not trusting him after that little stunt at breakfast.

I did all I could to keep him from taking over and lunging out, snapping Sasume's neck.

As I took Mitsuki upstairs, I could feel the heat coming from her as well as a strange scent on her that wasn't there before. Her eyes turned into a purple hue. As I laid her on the bed, I slowly crawled beside her kissing her softly, trying to distract her from the pains she was experiencing.

Sasume's expression was of worry and wonder as he stared down at her eyes. Not meaning to, I growled out at him as I hovered over her body.

"You need to let me see her. Can you step out for a while? Look, Giana will stay with me, so, no worries, ok?"

I looked over at Giana and at Sasume, and slowly nodded my head; I stood up, leaned over, and kissed Mitsuki on her temple then left the room. I actually was feeling anxious, so I decided it might be best to let Kaori run for a while. They looked after her.

••Sasume••

I watched as Shirou leaves out the door hearing his shift and leave through the back door. I looked down at my mate. Yes, this is my mate.

I'm not sure how this is possible or why it's happening with the three of us, but here we are. I'm not sure what or even how to tell

Shirou. Looking over at Giana, I confess to her.

Her eyes widened, looking over at me and then down at my beautiful mate. I let my hands caress her face and feel warm sparks through my hands and hear her let out a soft moan. Her eyes are a deep purple; it's a sign that she is definitely a part witch. I'm drawn into her like a crazed sailor to a siren.

The more I'm around her, the more I want to touch, her scent is intoxicating, and her eyes just pull me in.

I try to stay professional, but it seems pointless now I can no longer control myself leaning over and kissing her softly on the lips. I'm surprised when I feel her arms wrap around my neck as she kisses me back—hearing Giana gasp as she watches everything unfold. She whispers something in English as her eyes were closed, and she is sleeping, breathing fairly shallow but steady.

"Wow, how unexpected, or did you already have a thing for your nephews' mate?" She said in a snide way.

"I had a slight feeling of affection before; however, I wasn't completely sure if she was actually my mate until today, that is. This morning when I kissed her cheek, I was half playing and half experimenting.

Sure enough, when I kissed her, I felt a fantastic pull from her, and now it is really hard to stay away. I wonder if it has to do with having a combination of the fox spirit, witch, and wolf spirit that she holds inside.

I have never met anyone who held another spirit within oneself and lived long enough to tell the tale."

Giana shot him a worried glance. I don't know, but this is a very touchy situation that you are in with her and Shirou. I mean, don't you feel like a third wheel? Just as she says this, we hear a knock at the front door.

Knowing that Shirou would be the last one to be knocking, Giana looked at me and said she'd get the door.

Giana and Akifumi came waltzing back into the room; my eyes shot over to them as they both entered the room. Akifumi had a curious look at him as he kept coming closer to the bed, where Mitsuki was still sleeping.

His eyes changed color to his wolf blue hue. He was looking down at her, his wolf fighting to get out as he murmured the word Mate. "No, that's not possible!" I pushed him away, and he growled aggressively at me. He and Giana looked at me incredulously.

"How many mates can one girl have?" Giana asked.

"What do you mean, Giana? This is my mate, where did you find her?" Asked Akifumi.

"We didn't this is Shirou's mate, and you

and Romeo over here say she's your mate? This is one fucked up situation!"

As soon as she had her outburst, Shirou came rushing into the house; apparently, Giana had mind linked him to come back. As he opened the door, he looked at Akifumi and me then down at his mate. "What the hell are you two doing? Why are you both hovering over my mate?"

Giana took this as a time to escape but thought she should try to remove Mitsuki from the room.

That was a mistake on her part. When Shirou thought she was about to pick her up, he pushed her and the two of us away from her baring his canines at us with a guttural sound.

Now enter Hideaki, their father, and my older brother. He looks down at Mitsuki and sighs, then looks at the three of us and yell at us to leave the room while telling Giana to stay with her. "You three come with me now!"

••Takahashi, Hideaki••

It hasn't been but an hour since I came back with Akifumi; he was so damn excited to be back that he ran to Shirou's house when he asked Giana where she was. Not but 10 minutes later, I hear Giana practically screamingly me through a mind link to come over.

I let out a sigh and hurry over to his house, never a dull moment when I am here.

When I walk into the house, I hear growling, so I quickened my pace to where the racket was coming from. I shoved open the door and see the three of my boys; yes, even though my dad took in Sasume, he still is my son; it's just that the others don't know or realize that he is their brother. They see him as their uncle, who was weird for me.

So, each one is looking down at a young girl who is lying down on Shirou's bed, and Shirou continues to growl at the other two.

Not caring what is going on, I yell at all three to leave the room and follow me. They don't need to bother the girl who is sleeping. I gathered them downstairs.

"Ok, so what is going on?" Akifumi bursts out immediately.

"Dad, they found my mate!!" Shirou looked like he was about to commit murder as he let out a growl.

"She is definitely not yours; she belongs to no one but me!!"

I rolled my eyes as I tried to calm him down. "Well, we surely do have a problem now. How I see it, Mitsuki has three mates. Says Sasume.

"What do you mean three, Sasume!?" Well, I, too, recognize her as my mate. I think that because she has quite a mysterious background that we only know just barely the tip of who she truly is, Shirou."

"What is going on, and who is this girl, boys?" I asked them in a demanding tone.

"Her name is Mitsuki Takeda, and before you ask yes, she is from Seto Naika. My eyes widened as he tells me this girl, who is the equivalent to the human Yakuza, is lying upstairs and is near our pack.

I feel like I'm about to have a nervous breakdown. "What the hell is she doing here? Do you want them to come and start a damn war or something!?"

Sasume looked at me like I grew a third eye. He shook his head. "I don't think they are actively looking for her anymore.

I spoke to one of their pack members that I knew in college not too long ago, and it seemed like her parents knew she was ok. Now it was Shirou's turned to get riled up again as he started raising his voice at Sasume.

"I told you not to say a damn thing, and I didn't want us to be endangering her. What if the damn witches hear about her being here!?"

••Sasume••

"Witches, hmm, you know she has shown

that she has witch blood?" Her eyes turned a deep purple just earlier.

That's when I felt the pull, a change in her body. I felt super drawn to her earlier it was just a little hint, but now it's powerful like her soul is calling to me. I know and believe she is Shirou's mate; however, I definitely see that she is mine as well. It's taking all that's in me to stay down here with you." I look at my brother.

"So, what do we do now?"

"Ok, so let me get this right. She has many spirits within her, including having Majo blood?" Hideaki asks as I nod my head confirming what he had just said.
"Well, it makes sense with you as seeing that you also have Majo blood; your mother was half."
"What do you mean by that?" I asked him hurriedly. "Ok, well, there are things the three of you need to know now that it's coming down to all three of you have the same mate. You should know that you three are brothers.

I am your father, Sasume you don't share the same mother as Giana, Aki, and Shirou, but that is beside the point. Your grandfather took you away from your mother, who I had relations with for a short while.

He was worried things would go sideways in the pack for my actions, so he took you away from her after you were born and raised you as his own. As for the girl, we will have to check with the elders to see what is to be done with her as I don't know how three mates will work. I personally have never heard about this and am afraid of any who are rejected because of it. As the three of you know, it's not the best place to be on the rejecting end."

I stood there listening to what he had to say, looking at Shirou and Aki we all three probably had the same look on our face of disbelief as we were given this news so abruptly. "Please just get the elders here then. I think she is already suffering; she keeps losing consciousness, and I don't think she is going to last long like this."

It must have been a couple of hours later that we hear someone at the door, opening it we see some of the elders gathered. We welcomed them in and started explaining the situation.

A couple of them asked to see her, which the three of us got a defensive about but settled down and walked up the stairs so he could see her. I mind linked Giana to let her know we were coming up; she answered tiredly and opened the door, allowing all of us in.

I followed in after Shirou and looked over at Giana, who was sitting next to our sleeping mate.

When she sees two elders come in after Aki, she gets up off the bed and bows respectfully to them. They walked over towards her, and I had to restrain not only myself but my brothers from getting in between the elders and our mate. She stayed still sleeping in the bed as the elders looked over her closely examining her, one of the elders used to be the pack doctor before I took over; he had taught me many things.

I followed in behind him, looking down at Mitsuki, I see him check her eyes and heard him gasp when he saw her eyes, he then left the room and went back down to meet again with our father.

I leaned over and kissed her head then left her with Giana and Shirou, who was now sitting next to her. Aki came back down with me, followed by the last elder; as we approached father, we overhear the elder discussing passed multi-matings where there was more than one mate that had been able to stay mates.

He stated that the male mates must mark their mate at the same time so that there is no rejection. All mates must be in agreement with the arrangement.

He said that was the challenging part was everyone agreeing with sharing their mate. To save her from the pain she was in, and she had to be claimed and mated soon. He looked at Aki and me saying that our wolves will need to be actively in contact with her spirits to make sure that they will accept.

He said he would put us through a trance, so we needed to bring her down.

I mind linked Shirou to carry her down in no time he brought her down. The elders spoke with Shirou.

I could see that he was not happy about what they had to suggest but knew that this would be best to keep Mitsuki safe. I was definitely having trouble believing that Shirou would go along with this. It was easier for Aki and me because we weren't entirely wolf.

But for him, this would be the toughest for him and his (Alpha) wolf. We were all surrounding Mitsuki, all touching her body as some of the elders started chanting quietly in a different language.

I heard Giana say something about a witch chant, but I tried to stay calm and focus on letting my wolf take the reins.

黎 or Hajimu is my wolf's name taking from the darkness of his black fur. He was ready and has been more than reasonable, being the most reliable and patient alone.

He kept saying the name Kasumi over and over again excitedly, and he wasn't making it clear who this person was. My eyes were closed, but I had full vision of Mitsuki as well as

Inari, her fox, and Mizuki, her wolf. Further back, I kept following Hajimu.

He led me slowly to another girl. Her hair was similar to Mitsuki's, but instead of red, it was Black. Her eyes were a rich violet, and she stood quietly unmoving, unflinching, no fear whatsoever. She was absolutely divine. Hajimu rubbed his body up against her as I spoke to her. "What is your name, who are you?"

Unwavering, she spoke. "My name is Kasumi. I am Mitsuki's witch persona. She has many spirits within; however, I'm not that I'm more, and I know that you belong to me." She walked up to me and wrapped her arms around me, bringing me to her. You, too, are like me. I see you; I see the true you.

••Akifumi••

I have been jerked around since I first got back. I find my mate in my brother's house with my once called uncle, who I've just learned is my brother. I'm so freakin' confused and not sure what to think.

All I know is my wolf is screaming for his mate. I don't understand how it's possible or why I have to share my mate with my brothers. I was a little disappointed, but for some reason, it's not bothering me as much as one might think it would.

I had followed my brother around aimlessly, trying to find my place in all of this. I want to help our mate. I know she is not well. I can't wait to get the chance to talk with her and hope that she will like me.

As we gathered around, the elders had explained that each of us was going to allow our wolves free rein for a while so that they can reach their mate, who is in Mitsuki.

Akane, my wolf, had been pacing and nervously wanting to meet our mate. As soon as I closed my eyes, we walked up to Mitsuki.

Next to her was a small red fox; she looked gorgeous. I had never seen a red fox-like this in real life, so I was amazed at her beauty.

My wolf approached her, calling her name softly, so it's Inari ah such a cute name for a cute fox. I'm getting a feeling now I know why my wolf is such a small size compared to my brothers.

It was all for this little fox. It makes my heart warm to see them fit so nicely.

She seems so quiet, which my wolf is loving already. He continued to talk to her, and I could tell she was relaxed with him. While I approached Mitsuki, touching her face so very gently.

"Hi, I am Akifumi, and I hope you will accept me as one of your mates." Her smile is genuine and loving as she watched how comfortable Inari was with Akane—looking back at me with a gentle smile. "If Inari is happy, then I am most happy.

I am willing if all three of you are too. I really want to see Inari and Mizuki both happy.

"You are so sweet to think of them before yourself; what about you what will you be happy with for you?" I asked her pleadingly.

"This is for all of us. I can't imagine that this is so. I'm so happy that you already know each other it will make things easier right?" She asked me in the sweetest tone. "To be honest, I'm not sure if Shirou will feel the same. I know that Sasume and I will sacrifice our time with you, but I really don't know how he will be... we were told that we each have to mark you at the same time. Is that going to be too much? She blushes heavily at what I was bringing up.

"I have an idea from what Shirou explained to me earlier. I'm rather embarrassed to be in relations with all three of you at the same time."

"We will be gentle with you, well as much as we can," I say.

Leaning into her, I lower my lips to hers and kiss her gently, then feeling her kissing me back, I nearly lose my mind.

Getting swept into the moment, deepening our kiss and I slowly stop and pull away, looking down at her.

Smiling at her as I start to awaken from the trance, I see that all of us are coming to. She is still laying very still, and I turn to the elders to find out what has to be done next.

12

FOREVER OURS

She is still laying very still, and we turn to the elders to find out what has to be done next. One of the elders stepped up and rested her hand on Mitsuki's forehead with her own eyes closed. With a grim look, she turns to us.

"I'm guessing all three of you have officially met your mate. Now, this next step will be tricky; I'm hoping for your sakes that each of you has explained what you were supposed to, of what is to happen?
It will be painful if it is done incorrectly; if there is no strong will from any of you, then I cannot allow this to continue.

She has many abilities that we still do not understand, not only that, but she is connected strongly to each of you, so she will need all three of you.

You must put your differences aside and work together as her mates. If one part of her is hurt, the rest of the spirits will be affected.

She is one with them. You must really get to know her very well so that you can protect her. She is powerful but has many weaknesses, and not only that, but there is a dangerous coven that is looking for her, and we believe they are really close. When I look into her aura, I see a pulse that is being sent out when she is in this state. I believe that they are being reached out to. We mustn't let them get to her."

••Shirou••

"Oh, they won't have a chance," I say to the elder. I look at her and see similar purple eyes that most witches have. "So, you are a witch?" I asked.

"I am, but also a wolf, like Mitsuki; there were experimental things done to my mother before I was born.

However, I don't contain any other spirit other than witch and wolf. Believe it or not, this makes me and her safer for you to be around.

Pure witches have a curse that is brought upon them as they are born. That's why they carry a certain stigma and are the deadliest; however, the ones that carry a hybrid gene have been proven to be much stronger in magic, which is why they continue to mix our blood with theirs.

I'm thinking the reason why she is having

such a difficult time dealing with it must be because of the fox spirit she also holds."

We all nodded our heads as she talked about her condition and what it means for us as her mates; Mitsuki's eyes opened, showing a purple hue.

She began to move slowly and sit up. The pressure she is admitting around her was strong, and it began to be harder to breathe. "Whoever is the mate of the witch must go to her now and calm her down." Another elder said.

"What, I didn't think a witch would or could have a mate?" I asked in a surprised tone. I see Sasume rush to her side and take her hand in his, looking into her eyes and gently whispered into her ear and started petting her head with his free hand. (So that is why he said he too was a mate to her, that must mean Akifumi is a mate to Inari) I thought to myself.

I tried to listen to what he was whispering to her and caught only a little bit, as the pressure was reducing, so whatever he was saying, it was helping.

— (I kept hearing him call her Kasumi, so I'm guessing the witch to has her own identity no wonder she is losing her mind; it's like she has dissociative identity disorder). All the identities or spirits that she has in her must be struggling to be out and in control.

I approached them and knelt down beside

her, "are you ok, now?" I asked. She looked and me, and as she did, she looked exhausted. I felt so badly for her and hoped that we could all help get her back to being stable.

One of the elders started to speak in an urgent tone. "You must know that there will be trouble, possibly even a war against the puritans of America. I've been getting messages from the packs throughout all of Japan of sightings of congregations being formed between them and the majos here, I wasn't sure what it was then, but I know now that this really bad news for her as well as anyone protecting her.

If you three intend to be her true mates, you must make your claim soon, but as we have mentioned before, you must be careful and do it right. We will leave to give you time to figure out what the four of you decide to do.

Remember, she also has a say in what is to happen." As he finishes talking, the four of them turn away and walk out.

I turn back and look to Akifumi, who is still looking somewhat confused. "How did you do with Inari?" At my mentions of his mate, his eyes glistened, which gave me hope.

"She is so lovely and understanding. We talked about many things, and she wants to be with me, which makes me very happy. She is just so lovely and beautiful, Akane wants to be with her so very much, and I guess we know now why my wolf stayed rather small, so no jokes about him anymore!"

I smirked at his last statement; I'm just glad that she feels comfortable with him. She was rather timid around me and even bit the crap out of me too. I also had a long discussion with Mizuki while in a trance; I explained that I wasn't too happy with sharing Mitsuki and her with anyone.

She only reminded me that she was my mate and no others that it was Inari that had her own mate as well. It would only be Mitsuki that we would be truly sharing.

I still had a little trouble with, but since they are my brothers, I know she would never leave me; we will all stay here with our pack.

"I think it would be best if you two moved in here for a while, especially if we are to uh... well, mate her.

I said, rubbing my face in embarrassment. That's when I hear Gianna shout out at me. "Hey, you know that dad and I are still here, right?"

"Then you can leave no one is keeping you here," I said back to her. I got up and walked over to dad, "sorry for all of this and right when you just got back too."

He only nodded his head. "Well, now all three of my sons have found their mate. I'm just sorry they're within the same women. I hope you boys' figure this out and don't kill each other or that poor girl."

He said exasperatedly. He grabbed Giana, and they both left the four of us behind, shutting the door behind them. I turned to the other two. "Well, both of you will have to go get your clothing unless you just want to borrow mine for tonight.

We need to take her back upstairs, and we all need to have a talk. They all look at me, even Mitsuki, and say ok.

•• Mitsuki ••

You know when you sleep a long time, and when you finally wake up, you still feel exhausted and unrested? Well, that is currently my issue.

I get up and feel like I had been running miles and miles. I had a long talk with the three Naito brothers, who now I know are my mates; all three are very different.

Shirou is a serious and loving man showing a lot of power that he has inside himself, Sasume is a kind and gentleman who is thorough in sharing his feelings, which I find very different; and Akifumi is a funny, excitable, and very loving man too.

Their wolves love me to no end and would

do anything to be near me. All of them would protect me with no fear, which comforts me as well as Inari and Mizuki.

I am still getting to know Kasumi; she recently has been talking to me, but each time she does, it's causing migraines and soon after a blackout. My memory of her is always hazy, and I never remember much when she tries to communicate with me.

It's kind of frightening to not know when someone takes over, and I can't seem to remember anything; it's not like when Inari or Mizuki are given the control, I am kind of side seating my body with them in the lead.

When all three of us finally made it upstairs, Shirou wanted all of us to go to his room, which is the largest room in the house.

We all sat on the couch and waited for him to come back in. Each of the brothers sat on either side of me and held my hands in theirs.

My thoughts were still going wild about what we were going to decide on and how all of us would complete the bond and marking. Inari and Mizuki were so excited that each of them has met and agreed with their mates.

I get the feeling from them that Kasumi was also thrilled that she too had a man she could and would depend on and grow with.

I still am bewildered on the idea of three men loving me like this. Since I had never dated, much less had any previous relationships, I wasn't sure how this would work out. I just wanted everyone to be happy and satisfied.

Shirou walked in, smiling at me, and stiffly smiled at his brothers; I can see that this will be tough on him and Kaori. Being Alpha was hard enough; I'm guessing, and having to share a mate with his brothers must be straining and a trial for him.

Looking up at him, I felt my heart grow even warmer with his presence. He walked up to me and reached out his hands for me to take.

I placed my hands in his, and he slowly pulled me into his chest, wrapping his arms around me and taking in a deep breath before slowly exhaling and leaning down, kissing me lightly, raising both his hands firmly against my back.

Letting out a small moan into our kiss, I look down in embarrassment, feeling my cheeks getting warmer.

Shirou takes my hand, leading me to the bed, and looks to his brothers to follow us. They both stand up and move towards the large bed. Akifumi stands behind me, running his hand through my hair, gently lifting it from my shoulders, exposing the right shoulder. Lowering his lips and lightly starts kissing and nipping at my shoulder.

Sasume had climbed on the bed and approached the side of me, wrapping his arms around my waist and started kissing the side of my left ear while gently nibbling my lobe.

Shirou gently pressed up against me and pushed me slowly to the massive mattress; my head was guided to the pillow by Sasume as Shirou continued to climb up over me Akifumi also followed by climbing on to the bed and sat between my legs looking up at Shirou and me.

Sasume slowly lifted my blouse off as Shirou moved himself to the side of me. Akifumi unfastened my pants and slid them down and off, while Sasume kisses me once he has completely removed my top.

His kiss started off slow, but his tongue gently licks my bottom lip, and I opened my mouth for him to deepen his kiss our tongues were dancing together in our mouths both not in a dominating matter, but moving together lovingly.

At the same time, his gentle hands ran over my cheeks and gently tugged at my hair, I let out a small moan of pleasure.

I had felt my bra be unfastened and removed and suddenly being cupped by a set of warm hands, many kisses ran over my stomach and abs while I felt more kisses over my thighs.

This was the most overwhelming feeling I've ever felt in my life.

•• Third-person POV••

All the of the men were taken in by Mitsuki; they gave many kisses and moved around her lovingly petting her; Shirou switched places with Aki as he moved in between her legs.

He began to stimulate her slowly, placing his fingers over her opening. Aki took this opportunity to take pleasure in her by bringing her nipple into his mouth, gently nipping and suckling at her breast as he gently groped the other in his hand.
Sasume was kissing her deeply than kissed down her neck as she let out a gasp and small moan feeling absolute pleasure from each of them.

Sasume kisses his way to her other breast as he pushed Aki's hand away, his tongue playfully flicked against her nipple.

Shirou took both of her thighs into his arms

and gently pulled her down closer to him as he began to kiss the insides of her thighs, moving slowly every so often, nipping at her fleshy thighs closer and closer to her sex.

As he reaches to her warmth, his tongue flicks against her opening; she jumped a little as it had startled her and lets out a throatier groan feeling the pleasure of him intensify.

Her hands now in Aki's and Sasume's hair as they were closer, she began to lightly tug at their hair as Shirou licked and sucked on her more roughly as he moaned into her sex, sending vibrations through her allowing her to let out more pleasured sounds.

He removed himself after she had cum and crawled up her body, resting himself above her. She could feel the stiffness of his manhood through his pants as he looked down at her; she could see his wolf looking through them.

"I'm not sure I can hold off much longer, Mitsuki."

He said softly to her. "Then don't." She said in a gasp as Aki had nipped again at her breast.

Sitting up, he removed his clothes and looked to his brothers to do the same the other two followed suit and removed their clothing as well. All three were very swollen in excitement, and all looked at her like she was a feast to be had; but, Mitsuki wasn't scared for she wasn't alone.

Mizuki and Inari were there with her voicing their own excitement and pleasures of their mates and couldn't bare not doing anything more.

They each wanted to control and to take their mates for themselves; it was a mere torcher for them not to. With Aki and Sasume at her sides and now Shirou back above her, he leaned over kissing her lovingly before bringing himself at her entrance, pushing himself in slowly and passed her hymen, causing her to gasp out once more this time in discomfort.

He continued to kiss her more deeply now, not wanting her to think of the pain that she just experienced. He was unmoving until she seemed more relaxed.

He raised her up against him as he was still inside her. He backed out very little and pushed himself a little more each time as he started to move with more vigor, looking at his brothers to ready themselves, they got in place slightly behind her as he continued to now thrust himself into her, each of them kissed at her throat the two slightly from behind as Shirou was in front as she was also moving against him he could feel her clutching down on him his wolf was taking over giving that last word as they each bit down on her marking her simultaneously as they did the sheer intensity of it all had her weakened and finally blacking out.

They looked down at their mate lovingly, Shirou ordering the brothers to ready a warm bath to wash their mate in.

The two rushed and warmed a bath as Shirou brought in his naked mate; he sat down in the water having her body propped against his own, and each of them washed her body thoroughly with sponges, washing out her hair and rinsing her body Akifumi brought in a towel and gently wrapped her in it taking her unconscious body back to the bed laying her in the middle of it and crawling right next to her; he was startled as she began to move a little coming out of it she looked at him smiling before raising her eyes up at him their glow of gold and a slight purr from her as she wrapped her arms around him and laid her head against his chest.

They felt so blessed to have a mate like her. She was unique, beautiful, and so brilliant; she fit all of them so much. His face was beaming proudly as were Sasume and Shirou's.

•• Shirou ••

"Now she is ours; no one can take her from

us unless they want to die that is," I say, smiling to Aki and Sasume. We had spoken a long time while she laid there sleeping from exhaustion. All of us decided it was best if we took turns siring children.

I, as Alpha would be, first that was a given as then would lead to Sasume and then Akifumi as rank would show.

There would be no jealousies between us this way. She was free to spend time with whomever she wanted of us at whatever order at whatever time, just if we didn't go against each other's turn to sire.

We would explain this to her when she awakens fully to get her understanding and approval as well. That when it's not our turn, we may make love with her but with protection as to not mess with the order, and to keep our mates satisfied as well.

As the discussion between the three of us was over, I stood and left to talk with the pack. I was certain that my father and grandfather had already informed our pack of the situation that we were facing but hearing it from me would probably make things more of a realization.

13

INTRODUCTIONS

••Shirou••

"Okay, everyone, I am glad you have come to listen to me, your future Alpha. We have many things to go over. First of all, I want you to know that I have found my mate. At this time, she will be staying with my brothers and me. Yes, you have heard me correctly.

This is the next thing that needs to be mentioned; I want to introduce a person you all have known very well, our Doctor Sasame. I recently have learned the truth. He is my brother." The pack grew quiet, it really changes nothing, but other developments have come to pass.

When I found my mate, she came to me with a severe condition. I still want you to except your future, Luna. She is strong but comes with many enemies that are after her and her power. We must come together and protect her from these enemies, which like her, come from a foreign land. Sasume and Mitsuki, can you please come out with me now?"

My beautiful mate and my brother come and

join Akifumi and me. I place my hand on her back and draw her closer to me. I lower my face in the crook of her neck, inhaling her scent, which calmed my nerves.

Not seconds later, Sasame pulls me roughly away, causing me to growl furiously. "What the hell, brother?" I yelled at him angrily. He directed my eyes to her face and then stepped between us, still pissing my wolf off.

That's when Kasumi made her appearance; she grabbed Sasame's arm and leaned her face closer to his ear and whispered something causing him to nearly lose his cool.

"Majo! They are nearby; I need all the warriors to surround the perimeter now. The rest seek shelter below the packhouse."

Everyone moved quickly, getting to the places they were told. I told Sasame to get her down with the others; he looked at me a shook his head no.

My wolf was growing impatient with him, not understanding why the hell he wasn't listening to me. She turned to me and spoke in English.

Her eyes were dark purple, almost black and her veins around her eyes were more apparent. She looked back to where the pack once was. There was a man and a woman looking right at her.

Mitsuki, or rather Kasumi, who was in control, pushed me back with force behind her. I could see that her wolf was fighting to get out, but Kasumi, the Majo, was much more substantial. She raised her arms and closed her fists tightly.

When she opened them, she chanted something quietly and then releasing everything she had at the two unsuspecting majo.

They flew back when the force of her magic hit them. Keeping her hands outstretched and then pointed a finger to one of them bring him so high into the sky and then pulled her finger back, allowing him to fall with the gravity pulling him down faster, hitting limbs of the tree, he landed with a twisted back this Majo was now dead there was no saving him.

The other grew frightened of our mate as she directly pointed the finger at her then pointed at the floor next to her foot force had brought her to that spot very roughly.

She only looked at me, and then Sasume, he nodded and took control of the Majo. My grandfather, the acting Alpha, also stepped in and took control of her.

That's when Mitsuki's body was falling. I

wasn't sure why, but I grabbed her quickly before she could fall to the ground. She must have exhausted herself, and she will now need to recover.

I took her into the packhouse since it was closer than mine and took her to the top floor and to my old room in the house.

That was a lot of excitement for one evening. They picked a horrible time for a surprise attack. I am hoping that the pack will still accept her in as their future Luna. This is just abysmal timing.

☐

••Sasume••

As I heard my name mentioned with Mitsuki's, my heart grew warm and anxious. I was hoping that the pack would genuinely be accepting of the two of us and our new roles in the pack.

My hand wrapped around Mitsuki's hand, and I guided her out of the packhouse. Her long green silken dress was dragging on the ground, her wild red hair flowing freely. I am sure that the rest of the pack must have thought she was a spirit or something because of her beauty was remarkable.

We walked closer to Shirou; he wrapped his

arm around our mate, hugging her and taking in her scent. I was watching Mitsuki, who had been acting weird earlier she hadn't said anything for the last thirty minutes or so; I was worried that she was going to have another episode again.

When she turned to me, her eyes were dark purple. "They are here, and they want to kill!" When I heard her voice in my head, it was not like a mind-link, but a transference, it was very different, and it was Kasumi. "Shirou, something is wrong; we need to go!!" I said to him through the mind-link. I grew nervous and pulled Shirou back from her. He wouldn't or couldn't hear my mind-link.

I could see his wolf wanting to kill me as Kasumi grabbed my arm and leaned into me.

"The witches are here to kill everyone and take me! You need to protect the pack with your brother and get them out of here!!" She whispered into my ear. I looked at my brother, telling him the same he finally understood me "Majo!

They are nearby; I need all the warriors to surround the perimeter now. The rest seek shelter below the packhouse."

He then looked at me "Take Mitsuki down with the others and keep her out of this, hurry!" I shook my head. I knew that I could not make her go, and she was the only person that could deal with the Majo.

Kasumi had told me earlier that if we ever were to face them to let her deal with them herself and to not interfere.

She turned to Shirou. Her eyes were dark purple, almost black and her veins around her eyes were more apparent. ((English)) "The two will come, and one will die, another too from the richest rye."

My mind couldn't understand what she was meaning, but it looked like my grandfather understood her well. Once she was done, his wolf became in control, and he mind-linked the whole pack who were on the outer perimeter to look out for foreign Majo and to kill on sight, while he too had left the stage to the outer patrol.

When she turned back to where the pack once was, there was a man and a woman looking right at her. Kasumi, who was in control, pushed Shirou back with force behind her, as to protect him.

She chanted something; it was too quiet to make out from where I was standing, and the whipping of the wind did not help. Leaves, dirt, and other debris started lifting from the ground quickly. All of a sudden, I see one of the Majo fly up into the sky and then slam into every branch as he came crashing down to the ground.

His body mangled and twisted into many

different directions. The other Majo came flying at Kasumi and landed roughly at her feet; now, I understand this was her doing. Damn, she's powerful.

Kasumi looked at Shirou, and then at me, I looked to Shirou, seeing if he wanted this one as a prisoner. Yes, very much so, I could hear his mind-link; I nodded and took control of the Majo.

My grandfather, who I once called dad, had to come back in human form, grabbing the other side of the Majo. Both of us dragged the witch to the clinic. I still had some truth serum main ingredient Amobarbital, this one not only calms the one in question but makes their mind lucid. I'm hoping to find out why they are after her.

"Speak, Majo, and we know you can understand us!" This damn witch was trying to stay quiet. It looked as though she'd rather die than help us. She would not release any information.

Onimaru came up with the shocking device and plunged it into her side. Letting the current be a persuasion to talk since she wasn't in the mood to cooperate with us. The woman screamed out in pain as he pressed her again.

"Just tell me what it is you want with Mitsuki? Why are you after her?" It's been nearly an hour, and this damn Majo won't budge, not really knowing what to do next. This is not my expertise; I'm a doctor; I fix people, I don't break them down; however, when it comes to my mate, I am willing to do just about anything.

Just as Onimaru shoves the device against her side again, the door swings open, and Shirou walked in. I didn't see Kasumi or rather Mitsuki. "Where is our mate Shirou, who is watching over her now if you are here?"

He looked as tired as I felt; this whole thing was taking out the energy of our entire pack. Everyone is now on guard and leery of being left alone with a majo on the premises.

"She's with Giana and Akifumi and dad right now as she is still sleeping; I swear this damn condition of hers is making her sleep her life away." He said as he rubbed at his face, now glaring at the majo.

"Has she said anything yet? Not sure you would even catch a thing she said anyway, is Kaho back yet?"

Kaho is a pack member who spent time in London with the Sun Pack and can understand English fluently and really could be useful at a time like this since I wasn't so sure that this one could even understand Japanese.

Onimaru then spoke up. "Kaho is probably with his wife; she is near her due date now. I looked over to Onimaru with a relieved look.

"Well, at least we know he is still nearby;

can you go get him? This could go a lot smoother with him here. He nodded and left the room swiftly; I turned back to look at my brother as he hadn't stop glaring at the majo in front of him. "Who are you?" he asked as if I hadn't been trying this whole time to question her. She only glared back, not really showing that she knew what we were asking or even saying.

About twenty minutes pass and we see the door swing open once more, this time with Giana trailing behind Mitsuki, who, by the way, looks refreshed and pissed to no end, her eyes were glowing a golden hue. She marched up to the Majo and started talking or more like yelling at her in English.

Not understanding everything that was being said, we could only watch as she looked like she would torture this majo by herself. The girl looked shaken for a moment but then had a stubborn expression on her face.

Once I saw Mitsuki's eyes start to change into a purplish hue, I stepped in and tried calming her down. I didn't want her to exert herself again. Shirou was right. She was wearing herself down when Kasumi has the reins.

Moments later, we hear a knocking at the door; Shirou walked over, opening the door and allowing Kaho to come in; as he walked in, he took in the scene around him.

He didn't look too happy to be here and looked really bothered when he knew he had to talk to the Majo. He asked her many questions, which I'm assuming was the norm "what are you doing here, what do you want, and who the hell are you anyway?" kind of questions. She seemed surprised and started talking back to him; I was just hoping he was getting information that would be useful to us.

After talking to her for what seemed like forever, especially when you want answers like yesterday, he looked surprised and turned back and looked at Mitsuki, noticing the purple lingering in her eyes, while the Majo smirked knowingly.

•• Mitsuki ••

Waking up next to Shirou's worried glance as Giana walks into the room, I sit up feeling really refreshed and anew. "Is there something I can eat; I'm feeling so hungry right now," I say, facing Shirou.

"Uh, yes, Mitsu. I'll be right back." He says as he rushes out the door. Giana came and sat in front of me and began talking to me.

"So, do you know who these people are?" She asked in curiosity. I shook my head. "I first learned of them a couple of years ago when I was forced to leave my family, and then again not too long ago after I left Tokyo.

They have been following me since. I know

that they want to use me for something, and I can assure you that it's nothing good.

I'm now getting the feeling like they are trying to start a war, pinning all supernaturals against each other. Not only are they planning a war but having a feeling from Kasumi that they are designing weapons through different hybrids with Witch blood or something. She thinks that they are trying to control her, but she is too strong."

When I finish talking is when Shirou comes into the room carrying a tray of food. Placing the tray next to me on a table, he looks at the two of us kindly.

"After you eat, I would like for you if you feel ready to talk to the witch; I am getting told that she is either being difficult or simply just doesn't understand what is being asked of her.

We really need to know what that is planning against us and why they want you so badly.

Some time had passed in silence as I was eating and thinking to myself and quietly in my own head with Mizuki and Inari going over everything that we all have learned, knowing that it wasn't the whole picture, we would have to talk to Kasumi as well which wasn't easy at all, when talking to her I tend to get severe headaches and always feel like I am losing control.

She is always bringing up Sasame; she had told me that he was also a witch or part witch anyway; she said when she is near him, she feels at her most vital, and that the only way to be stronger is to waken the majo within him.

This was again too much for me to truly understand, but I didn't argue with her. I mean, she is me in a sense, and how can one argue with oneself?

When I was finished eating and deliberating with my inner spirits, I looked at Giana and Shirou, who were quietly talking to each other this whole time, not bothering me.

They probably felt that I was talking to them, so I decided it was best to give me time to myself. I wonder if they too have chats with their wolf at times?

With me, it's like I am having a whole council meeting between a wolf, fox, human, and witch. Noticing that I was watching them, they both stopped talking and looked at me.

"So, are you ready?" Shirou asked in interest, nodding my head, I stood up. He walked over and took my hand in his, kissing the back of it and looking at me.

"You know you are not alone; you have me, Giana, my brothers, and the whole pack too. We will stand by you and help the best we can as a pack. You are a part of our family now."

Feeling his hands wrap around my waist now standing in front of me and looking down into my eyes, I could see his sincerity nodding my head; I wrapped my arms around his back, feeling his warmth.

He too brought me in closer to him, his face buried into my neck, inhaling my scent, making a low sound sounding like a grunt.

Turning my head to face him, our noses brushed against each other, his eyes catching my own as he brushed his lips softly against mine, surprised at his actions but not disappointed, I leaned more into his kiss, tilting my head, feeling his hands brush against my face and wind up in my hair kissing my lips with more vigor.

I lost myself in his kiss, and he must have too until we heard a cough of Giana trying to get our attention. "Must be nice to slip into your own little world, but it's time to be in this one. I'm afraid we need to go to Sasame now."

She said with urgency. We both looked at her and nodded, separating from each other.

As we are walking to the clinic, which is further into the home near the basement, I am feeling extremely pissed off; these witches have been doing nothing but pissing me off.

They have basically chased me all the way here to Shizouka, not sure how they keep finding me either so damn annoying.

I feel the presence of Kasumi demanding to be in control, me knowing that this is probably the best choice, I mentally asked her to take it easy so that she doesn't take all my strength again.

She must have convinced the other two since I didn't hear Mizuki nor Inari complaining about it. Their distaste for being near the witches was clear although they didn't mind Kasumi, which is a relief not sure how insane I would get if I always had squabbling going on in my damn head, it's bad enough for me now with the knowledge of having the three of them in the first place.

We reached the door, and Shirou opened it, allowing myself and Giana to enter; the scenery looked of the one you might see in a movie or something. The room was lit up with fluorescent lights hanging overhead. There was pretty much everything that you would see in a hospital room and more.

As I looked over at the witch, I felt anger from all three within, but I am sure that at this moment, Mizuki must have shown her face feeling an extra amount of rage as I rushed at the witch.

"Who the hell do you think you are; how long have you been following me? If you don't start talking now, I will let my spirits take turns tearing you to shreds!"

All of a sudden, feeling nothing but pure rage as I heard Kasumi's voice overlap my own feeling, an immense power overcome me; I grabbed the witch's hair pulling it back, forcing her to look at me.

Her eyes are widening at first; she could see

my eyes clearly, seeing that my witch spirit had full control now. "Kasumi, hey, can you look at me. Hmm? Look here, come talk to me."

I heard Sasame in the most calming voice. I looked at him and slowly backed off. He led me to the corner behind the shelving and caressed my arms soothingly, still talking to me gently, trying to calm the rage.

Moments later, Kaho walked in, looking around the room with a very pissed expression; this witch was fucking up everyone's damn day. Sometime before Kaho came into the room, I noticed that Giana had left the room, Kaho had passed where I was standing, and as he walked over to the witch, he started firing off a load of questions.

She seemed surprised and started talking back to him. At the same time, Sasume petted my hair soothingly and kissing my forehead, trying to reason with Kasumi.

I noticed Kaho look at me with a very surprised expression while he was talking to her and talking to her in a calmer voice now, still looking in between the two of us, seemingly starting to get the grasp that I too had a witch within me.

She only had a stupid grin on her face like she won something as she looked back at Kaho. Shirou walked up to them and started talking to Kaho.

I couldn't really hear what they were saying,

though, since his back faced me and so I could no longer hear them or see their lips moving. Then Shirou walked out of the room. Sasume held me closer, rubbing my back.

I started feeling more at ease with his presence and the love that he showed towards me.

I then heard something that I didn't expect from her lips; she mentioned a name, Lacy Black while talking to Kaho. My eyes, I'm sure must have been something else because when Sasume looked into my eyes, he gasped and tried to hold onto me.

I inadvertently pushed Sasume out of the way, sending his body slamming into the ground hard, my body launching into the air shifting as I landed onto the witch; she no longer had a smile on her face.

I felt my jaws close down on her neck, you must have guessed it, but it was Mizuki that came out of a shift and perched upon this lousy witch. Kasumi and Mizuki were working together and were in complete control of everything.

•• Third-person POV••

Everything erupted into chaos; there was the blood that was sprayed from the witch, surprising Kaho as well as Sasume, who still crouched on the ground; his wolf, scratching at the seams to get out. Sasume could only see red as he finally let Hajimu go; entirely in control, he rubbed his body up against Mizuki, who was sporting Kasumi's purple eyes. They have never seen a wolf with witch eyes; it's so very eerie. She turned to look at Hajima and started to relax, seeing that the witch was dead now, and there was no longer a threat. Sighing, she shifted back and leaned up against the wall, sinking slowly to the ground; Hajima looked up at her, now content that she was calm, and licked her face making her smile. Running her hands through his fur, Kaho looks on with raised eyebrows letting out a deep sigh. "Well, looks like I'm done here?" he says, turning around and walks out the room happy to get back to his mate. Sasume slowly shifted back, grabbing his white coat off of a coat hanger, slipping it on, and looked up at her as she placed her hand on his face looking back at him tenderly. He was relieved as she didn't seem bothered by him being partially nude. He sighed in relief and looked down at his lovely mate.

••Sasume••

I could only stare at her in awe, her eyes still in a stunning purplish hue. I can't believe how in control and how well Kasumi works with Mizuki on keeping Mitsuki and Inari safe.

Genuinely inspiring and shows that not all witches are horrible, that some should be feared, but also revered, especially my Kasumi, my beloved mate.

Feeling this, I can't help myself leaning into her and capturing her lips softly at first, then more hungrily as she reciprocates her desires to me. Her arms wrap around my neck as she kisses me deeply; I ran my hands through her tousled black hair, tugging her closer to me as she pulls me tightly to her; I was lost in her, completely lost. She then pulled away from me, allowing us to catch our breaths; slowly closing her eyes, she softly sighs, getting herself up and looking at me to follow her.

As she brought her hands over her face and down her hair, everything seemed like a mirage.

First, her eyes changing back to the deep greens of the forest and then the soft red curls of her hair, Mitsuki was back, smiling at me; it is so strange that our mate can have such different appearances not only with her fox and wolf forms but as her witch persona as well.

The powers she possesses is extraordinary and unheard of. It's no wonder they want her so badly.

14

ANSWERS

•• Mitsuki••

While walking with Sasume, my mind drifts back to when I was in his arms, my cheeks flushed even though Kasumi was still in control at the time, I was fully aware of the intimacy between the two of us, or three?

It's so confusing now that I am entirely connected, well mentally anyway, to Inari and Mizuki. Still, when I think of Kasumi, I am so unsure of everything since she was hidden away from me until now.

She had told me that it was Sasume that had brought her forward and finally out.

His blood called to hers just as Shirou and Kaori had called out to Mizuki. I am so overwhelmed at times, but I have noticed when comforted by any of the three brothers, my nerves nullify; I become chilled and collected. I feel so loved and wanted by them; it really is a new feeling for us.

My mind slowly drifts off, thinking of the witch and her slip up of Lacy Black. I have the urge to want to talk to my mom. I feel as though there are things that haven't been said by my mom. As I walk back with Sasume, I slip my hand softly into his; he gladly accepts my hand and gently squeezes it. "So, how are you doing now? I can tell that you have much on your mind." Sasume says as we leave the clinic.

"Oh? you mean when the witch brought up something strange or when Kasumi and Mizuki drained her?" I said. It wasn't snarky, more like exhausted. I was just put out with everything continuously happening all at once. I mean, can a girl catch her breath? Sasume let out a sigh and nodded his head.

"I know what you mean. I would love to just spend time with you without feeling like someone is after you. We are warriors, well, not me. I'm the doctor, but we have trained to defend. Nothing will ever happen to you, although I don't think we have to worry too much about that either; you're powerful, you know that, right?" As he said this, he pulled me to a stop and looked at me, taking my other hand in his.

Looking up at him, I shook my head; "I get it, but I'm not sure what exactly I should be doing. I just got here, and now I have three important men in my life. It's a lot to take in, and I am afraid I'll either do something wrong or miss something entirely."

Sasume pulled me into him, wrapping me into his firm body, so warm and strong. He puts my mind at ease once again. I am shocked when I feel another warm body from behind.

Looking over my shoulder, I see Akifumi smiling down at me, then leaning down, sniffing at my neck. "You need to get that women's scent off you, come on, let us walk you to the bathhouse.

They must have cleared out the bathhouse; the only person there was Shirou. He must have been waiting for us to get in. Walking over towards me with a saddened expression on his face, he started to remove the blood-soaked articles of clothing from my body.

"How did you manage to get so much blood on you anyway?" asked Shirou. I looked back around at Sasume and shrugged my shoulders up.

"uh, I don't know, I guess when I shifted, the blood must have transferred back onto my clothes? I said, merely blinking my eyes up at him.

He turned towards Sasume with a surprised expression expecting to get a better explanation from him about what exactly happened. Sasume ran his hand through his hair and explained in more detail what had happened,"and that's not even the full of it. Apparently, Mitsuki can shift without shredding her clothing."

Shirou's eyebrows arched. He was gently wiping my chin, which must still have blood on it with his thumb.

Then taking my hand and guided me into the shower. He and Akifume started taking my clothes off, probably checking for any wounds left behind from the witch.

I guess they didn't understand that the witch didn't even get the chance to harm me when Mizuki took over and killed her; that's all I could think about of while they were undressing me; Sasume had turned on the water, and I slowly walked in the stall letting the water pour over my head.

He came in after me with a washcloth and soap. I sat on the stool as he kneeled down behind me, wiping my body down.

My mood was very solemn; I had many thoughts swarming my mind. It seemed never-ending, having thoughts like my mother came in mind; I know I have to contact her now.

Sasume now started lathering shampoo in my hair. I leaned into him, letting my eyes closed.

Thinking back, I don't like that the witch was saying that I am connected to a woman with the name of Lacey Black; I had heard about her before back at my parent's estate.

I wonder if she is a witch or something? My mother had warned me of the witches; I just wish she would have told me what they wanted me for.

They were only murmurs never really directed at me, and at the time, I wasn't interested as I had many other things that I felt was more important, but now I wish I had shown more interest in what my family did.

I was so focused on getting away and my future with education rehearsed. It's time to play catch up with my family, and now that I know that my parents are hiding a lot from me.

Once Sasume had finished rinsing my hair, we both got up, and we dressed and walked back to Shirou's home.

I am now the upcoming Luna for the Warrior Pack. I can't afford to be ignorant of what is happening around me any longer.

After deliberating with myself for some time, I decided to start to ask questions.

The first people that I will talk to will be the Alpha, then I will talk to my mates, they all seem to know much more than I do, and now that will change.

As I walked into the house, I was greeted by Shirou first with a long kiss, and he nearly stole my breath; as I came back up for air. I let out a giggle and smiled up at him.

"I need to talk with your grandfather and father tomorrow. There is much to discuss. The witch had mentioned a name that rang quite a bell with me.

I have heard things around my family, and I know that they have been keeping something from me, and I need to find out why. So, I will need an audience with not only your family but mine as well."

At that moment, Akifumi and Sasume both

were listening in.

"I just asked our father, and he has time in the morning to talk with us, he won't be too happy to see your family, though," Akifumi said. "Should I be worried?" I asked, not sure what my family could have done to theirs.

"No, not really; I am not sure how to explain this," he said, looking back at his brothers to help him. Sasume came to his rescue, "so, the rest of our community sees your family as a threat of sorts.

They are quite influential in the world order; they are known to end things or make things disappear for the lower empire.

Several groups think that they have had dealings with several of the organized crime syndicates, including the human Yakuza group, although there is no proof of this. They are called the Koroshi-ya Okami no mure."

After this initial blow, Sasume rested his hands on my shoulders. My eyes widened to the name of my family. I still couldn't believe it, not at all. How could they keep this from me?

I only knew my parents had business trips that included lots of travel.

To think they originally wanted me to stay with them in their business. As the news came down on me like a ton of bricks, I dropped down into the chair that was in the kitchen. Resting my head in my hands and heavily sighed.

"So, you can see why our father would be a little leary to invite them to our lands?" Shirou asked. I nodded my head. I was starting to feel overwhelmed with all of the new information. "Will all of you stay with me when I confront them? I will have to ask so many questions about this new information that has come up.

I am not sure how to go on from here, not knowing if I am on opposing sides. I would like to have my family and your family as one.

There has to be understanding between the two now that I am tied to you as my mates. With this, we all were in agreement; we all went upstairs.

I was nervous about my family; the old and the new it was like a perfect storm. I usually am reckless or impulsive about things; now, I have to think of others, not just myself.

Shirou led us into his room, pulling my hand, leading me into his bed. The others crawled around me as I laid down. It was nice in our puppy pile.

We are all gathered in the Alphas office; thankfully, it is a relatively decent sized room. I wanted to speak to the Alpha by myself at first but then grabbed Shirou's hand in a panic. I guess I am not that brave yet. I thought to myself as I looked at the over-sized man sitting at his desk.

He looked scarier than my father, who is an Alpha himself. And I was to believe that this man was, for better words, scared of my father?

"Hello, Mr. Naito. I want to discuss somethings in advance before my parents arrive. I would like you to know that I did not know about werewolves or kitsune nor witches; this is new to me.

I had changed when I was much younger into a fox, but those memories were taken from me by Inari and Mizuki. They had hidden inside to protect me until I had the protection of our mates."

He only looked at me as I vomited all of this information out on him. His thick grey eyebrows were in his hairline. His hands were brought together and propped under his chin as he looked at me in thought.

He wasn't in a hurry and thought things through, better than myself; I could tell he was very wise and didn't look too judgmental of me, which was reassuring.

Shirou wrapped me into his arms, resting his face on my shoulder, and gave a small kiss to my neck. I know my wolf was in heaven, but Inari and I were freaking out horribly; I couldn't believe he was doing this in front of the Alpha. Future Luna or not, I was not ready for public displays at all. I felt my face on fire; my eyes widened, and started feeling panicky.

I'm not sure if that was my feelings of insecurities or if they were Inari's. The Alpha smirked at his son and his spooked mate; he could see the fox's glow showing through Mitsuki's eyes.

Realizing that she was just below the surface, he made sure to talk without too much force. -"I understand some of what you are saying and in no way hold you responsible for what happened last night.

You actually took care of most of the issues yourself. You are quite the find, so powerful. I would never harm my son's lovely mate, either; you have no reason to fear me, little fox. So, your parents will be here soon. I hear that not only did your family not tell you about shifters, but they withheld what their livelihood is as well?" he asked in disbelief—running his hand through his hair, with a slight grimace.

I had a frown on my face as I nodded my head. "I hate that they lied to me, my whole life, I didn't care if they were trying to protect me. I think that they put me in more danger because I didn't know."

Just as I spoke, there was a knock at the door," come in," the Alpha barked out.

He seemed tense, and his eyes started to change. His wolf must be close to coming out for the first time. I could actually taste fear in the room, though I couldn't tell if it was mine, his, or Shirou's. When the door opened, my father, mother, and his nephew Shiro came through it.

I knew then that answers were about to come to light, might not be everything, but we would be getting some.

My father stood straight and tall, looking in charge, and for the first time, I could see why others might be afraid of him. He had a powerful aura. My mother looked at me and rushed to me but stopped short when she noticed Shirou's protective stance next to mine.

I felt his arms tighten around me like he was afraid someone would take me from him. Mother looked at him and then at me with a shocked expression at first, then she had a big smile on her face.

"Mitsuki, do you finally have your fox now?" she asked sincerely.

••Luna Takeda••

It was late at night when we got the call to come to the warrior pack down in Shizuoka; their Beta Takeda sounded nervous, but still with respect as I would expect from other packs.

They were still afraid of Mitsuo, it seems. I called in my mate and let him know that Mitsuki was with the Warrior Pack; his hackles seemed raised.

I was surprised as well, as I thought she

wouldn't really fit into a wolf pack of any kind. Her fox had been flighty when she was younger. I had a fear that maybe they had imprisoned her.

Their Beta didn't disclose anything other than that Mitsuki was there and that their Alpha requested an audience with us as soon as possible.

Mitsuo was furious after hearing me relay what I was told. Growling, his hands balled up in fists. "We need to leave now!

I will not have our daughter prisoned by anyone; she must be frightened. I know that little fox will not last long there.

They must know what she is by now, and that can't be good if they think they will use her as a bargaining chip for anything." He said in a fury.

We left in a hurry; there was Mitsuo, our Beta Shiro, and I; it took us most the night to run up there in our wolf forms carrying bags of clothing in our mouths.

It was early in the morning when we finally came into the warrior packs domain; we felt a push as we entered the threshold of their territory, and we headed past the Sunpu Castle. As we passed the castle, several of the wolves of the warrior pack met up with us then guided us to the main house.

Before coming into the manor, we had changed back into our human forms, getting dressed, and following Takeda into the home.

As the door open, Mitsuo stood in the way I could feel him exerting power towards the other Alpha; I looked around him.

As I spotted Mitsuki, I pushed passed him and straight to her, stopping just in front of her when I noticed a man holding onto her; at first, I thought it was against her will, but looking closer, I could tell he was claiming her as his own.

I couldn't help but be happy for her as I knew now that she was his mate and that he was delighted with her even being a fox; it was definitely strange but not unheard of.

"Mitsuki, do you finally have your fox now?" I asked. "I do and a wolf and a witch." She stated exasperatedly. I stood there in shock as Mitsuo started pushing closer to her.

That's when her mate pushed her entirely behind him. "You aren't taking her anywhere; she's mine!" he shouted in fear.

Everything seems to turn upside down as two more men came into the room and rushed to Mitsuki's side, blocking her from Mitsuo, as if he would ever hurt her. She was his prized child.

Before it escalated anymore than it already had, Alpha Naito stood from his chair and growled at all of the men in the room. "I will have no fighting in my office. You were called in to talk with your daughter. No one here will hurt her, especially not her mates.

"Her mates? As in more than one?!" Mitsuo exclaimed. "Yes, my mates. I hear Mitsuki say in a heavy sigh as she pushes her way through them.

I think we all need to sit and calm down before someone gets hurt unintentionally. She seems so strong surrounded by her mates, or is it just because she has her others to lean on?

She walked over to the couch and sat down, looking at the rest of us to sit as well.

Who I am assuming are her mates sit around her on the sofa. "How about we start this over again with introductions?" I asked her. She nodded, looking relieved.

"Yes, I think that is best. Guys, this is my mother, Takeda Nanami, and my father, Takeda Mitsuo. As you have told me, they are the Alpha and Luna of the Koroshi-ya Pack?" she looks at us in question with a little irritation, which I can understand since we never explained much to her.

We never told her since her first shift to her fox we were cautious about what we told her.

"Yes, that is correct. I see that your mates have explained things to you, but I still don't understand three mates, Mitsuki?"

Mitsuki took two of her mates hands in hers and smiled at all three of them.

"Well, first off, they are all sons of Alpha Naito, this is their pack doctor and my mate Sasume, their future Alpha Shirou and the future Beta Akifume, both also my mates. I am marked by all three; Inari, my fox, is finally happy with Aki as well as the other two you have not met yet.

My wolf Mizuki is Shirou's mate, and Kasumi also has claimed Sasume."

She had pointed to each of them, and when she mentioned each on, they seemed to beam with pride, which made me so happy.

Mitsuo didn't miss how she didn't state that Kasumi must be the witch in her; I am surprised that even witches would have claimed mates.

It made me wonder about the doctor's attributes and what she is not sharing; I think I will leave it alone for now and not stir the proverbial pot for now.

••Alpha Takeda••

I felt like I was going to demolish this whole damn pack. I can't believe they kept all of this from me. I turned and glared at their damn alpha.

He is still standing trying to exert his damn power over mine as if he could possibly win over me; I can't even stand the thought of my daughter surrounded by these damn mongrels.

Our family has always had issues fighting

over providences for over centuries. Since before the Sengoku period and they still stand so proud since before Oda Nobunaga himself.

I am trying my best not to kill them. I can see that my daughter is very much happy with the three of them; how can the gods hate me so much as to have three of the Naito family thrusted into my family now.

"Look, I know our families haven't ever seen eye to eye, but with this new development, I think we should all try for Mitsuki's sake.

I can see that you care for her; I cannot picture a world that I could never see her. I want to invoke a peace treaty between the two families for now."

I look to Alpha Naito, and he rose to his feet and walked over; his body seemed more relaxed now, and he held a bow until I too bowed to him.

The tension in the room dropped suddenly, making everyone more comfortable I looked over at my Luna as she gave a small nod.

"My son Shirou will be taking over as Alpha now that he has found his mate. He already made the official announcement last night. What we need to discuss are the witches and why they are after our Luna, your daughter. All we have gathered so far is that they are from Beikoku, or as what they call America. Nanami walked up beside me, facing the Alpha, and took my hand, mind-linking to me that it was time for us to bring forth the history of Mitsuki.

She then turned to Mitsuki since this was her story she needed to know, it was time.

"Mitsuki, as you know, you were born in America; your mother still lives as the Luna in Washington state.

Her name is Lacy Willard. She was once Lacy Black when she was mated to Alpha Black of the Red Moon Pack until he was killed during the witches' invasion.

During this attack on their pack, your mother was taken, and she said that they had done things to her.

She didn't go into detail, but I am sure it was nothing good. After you were born, you were exhibiting special powers, and your eyes had scared the Luna, and she thought you to be cursed as a witch and didn't want to endanger the pack or your twin brother." She explained sorrowfully.

"I have a brother?" Mitsuki asked, her eyes wide, shocked by the news. Sasume wrapped his arm around her, letting her tuck her face into his neck.

"Do you think they will talk to me? Does my brother know about me at all?" She turned from Sasume's neck and looked at me, her eyes filled with tears.

"We could always invite them here if they do know; if not, I think you might want to let them know." Alpha Naito said gruffly.

"I have updated Luna Willard on what has happened recently, we have business dealings that I can't discuss with you, but we can see if Zachery, your brother, has even been told of you.

I think it would be suitable for you and your wolf to see your bother and his wolf.

It will help mend and complete you. I can't guarantee that she would agree or not, but I am sure Zachery will want to meet you; he always acts like something is missing, even with him not meeting his mate yet."

I told her. Finally, I see a smile from her. I only hope that they both agree to come to visit since her mates and I wouldn't let her leave

Japan with the witches still at large.

"We have a room in the manor. If you want to rest up before tomorrow, I think it would be best to set up a teleconference with the Blood Moon Pack soon though they should be up now.

15

One Big Happy Family

••Alpha Willard••

When the phone rings, I roll over my beautiful sleeping mate; it's early in the morning, and we've slept in compared to when we would typically get up. Today it was the ringing of the office phone that's wired to our room.

The shrill ringing it's driving my body into getting up; I have debated to disconnect it because of moments like this; we had been up late in a pack meeting.

I was hoping to sleep more, but, as Alpha, I can't. As I answer the phone, I am surprised to hear Alph Takeda on the other end. His English has gotten much better in the twenty or so years I have known him.

I got off the phone with him and woke up my mate and letting her know that we would be taking Zachery to Japan. This was a trip well overdue. I choose not to give her too many details since I have a feeling she would not want to go.

I feel as though she owes it to herself and her children. They are grown up now, but they need the opportunity to meet one another after all this time.

I feel bad for Zachery as he had always wanted to meet his sister; after he found out about her about a year ago when the witches came here looking for her.

I went ahead and let the Beta know as well as Zachery, warning them not to say anything to Lacy about it. Our Beta, Rick, had thought that it was a bad idea not to tell her, thinking it might be too much of a shock to see Mitsuki, her daughter.

I was persistent; I felt that I come to know her better than most, and she never really expressed out loud that she wanted to see her daughter.

I know she was always listening in to calls that we got from Japan and had asked me about her when no one was listening in. so I sent everyone off in preparation for the trip. We are going to Japan. There were three of us going leaving Beta Rick and his mate in charge while we were away; I wasn't sure how long we would be gone but really didn't mind getting away for a while.

We left near the afternoon in a privet jet arranged by the Washington State council. The Alpha or Luna of the Senshi Pack must have called them, letting them know that we were going to meet up with them because, as we arrived, everything was set, as there was no need for an appointment with the council.

It took us approximately 10 hours to Tokyo and another four hours from there to Shizouka. So needless to say, we were worn out by the time of our arrival.

I was lucky that the acting Alpha came to greet us instead of Mitsuki or one of her mates, as I don't think that would have been the smartest move right away.

We rode in silence as we were pretty exhausted, and it was already pressing at five o'clock in the evening. It took a short time to arrive at their pack establishment, which was very impressive.

I had done my history check on the local area, finding that there was a castle nearby that I know that Lucy would like to see as she enjoyed the aesthetics of the castles and culture of Japan.

"So, Alpha Naito, I hear that there is a castle nearby?" from the review mirror, I notice the Alphas eyebrows rise, and Lucy perked up to the news, which made me smile.

"Ah, yes, our family has maintained the Sunpu Castle for many centuries now." He said with a longing look.

"Hmm, was your family at odds with the Shingen clan than?" Lacy asked, beaming curiosity.

"Yes, and now both families have actually called a truce just recently due to opposing sides finding their mates. It brings relief to the two packs to finally be at peace.

I am guessing Tsuki Omi has set things straight for once and for all." Says the Alpha in a relaxed tone. With his reply, I could see happiness in her features; this was good.

She needed to see the goodness in this whole situation; I was hoping that the discussion would happen like this. I knew her best, after all. She would see the benefits of both families that Mitsuki has brought them by being sent here.

I realized not that long ago that she did feel guilt for sending her daughter away; but, this is what needed to happen to mend two families even if she didn't know that Mitsuki is the reason for all of these positive reactions.

I would not stand for her to tear herself up over it. The Takeda family has done tons for Mitsuki by giving her a future, and now her mates that she might not have found until much later.

The Alpha pulled through the gates we passed cute Japanese style homes. Some of them had one-story flats and other two-story flats. They seemed so stylish and in between modern and old style.

••Zachery Black••

When the Alpha had mentioned that I would have a chance to see my sister, who I had just recently learned about, I nearly jumped out of my skin in a rush to see her.

I hadn't understood why I felt incomplete, pieces of my heart seem to be missing while I was growing up, and I wanted to mend them.

Only then could I find my mate, or at least that is what I think.

I couldn't control anything, especially when most of this happened when we were infants. Now I have the opportunity of a lifetime to go to Japan and to meet my sister finally.

The flight was a long one; I was able to reflect I really wanted to talk to my mother, but had made a promise to father not to mention seeing Mitsuki.

When I heard that I had a sister, I was surprised to learn that she was in Japan and lived a life there.

I was distraught that my mother sent her away and didn't understand the reasons why. What could she have done wrong as an infant? I chose to let these things go, for now, now that I will meet her, I no longer care to know her excuses. I don't want to despise my mother, so I will let this shit go for now.

Then we stepped out of the plane; I assume it was Alpha Naito that met up with us; he kept looking between my mother and me, his eyes narrowed a little at my mother but kept a friendly disposition between my father and me.

I could tell he was trying to figure out what my mother's story was; I heard that my sister had met her mates in this Pack and that she had three of them, which is not normal.

We usually have only a destined mate, but from what I heard that my sister had something special about her, my father said it was their story to tell, talking about my mother and sister, from the tone he used, it didn't sound like a pleasant story at all.

He did say that Mitsuki was a remarkable person now the future Luna, similar to me, as the future Alpha to our Pack.

The Alpha pulled through the gates we passed the Japanese style homes. As we approached what I was guessing the main house, I saw a small woman come out with two other men.

She looked so much like my mother; it was uncanny. Her red hair was a touch lighter in color, but still, the same hue that my mother and I had. Curls reached down her slender body, and her eyes were a darker shade of my own, an intense forest green.

As she walked to the vehicle, she smiled though it seemed a little forced. I looked over at my mother, but she was to busy focusing around the estate; children played all around, kicking soccer balls and pushing at each other, playfully passing the vehicles, and into another gated area.

I quickly got out of the car, rushing towards her, stupidly a little too quickly as I must have alerted her mate, as he quickly moved in front of her. Once I abruptly stopped, I saw her peeking around her mate, and her eyes were catching an exciting whirl of colors like a kaleidoscope deep greens, golds, and slips of blue or silver; it was hard to tell when they seem to be continually moving.

I think something must have clicked with her because not even a second later, I was getting attacked by her, not aggressively, no, just tons of hugs, and while she clung herself onto me, nothing could shock me more.

My wolf had recognized his sister, and I could feel the hum of contentment and happiness from him; this was one of the missing pieces for sure.

That's when we heard a gasp behind us; Mom, I knew she must be surprised by all of this, I felt a little guilty about knowing that I would see my sister, but I also found relief. I have been deprived of her my whole life, and my wolf was so happy now.

Mitsuki finally backed off of me and smiled sheepishly up at me, her cheeks held a cute red tint to them as she grabbed my arm and moved me toward her mate.

Just as we were being introduced, I see my longtime friend pop his head from behind the door and had a shocked expression on his face. Sasume came out in a hurry and scratched behind his neck in awe.

"I don't know how I didn't put the two together. Who knew that my mate was your sister? Tsuki Omi must be having her fun with us as it truly is fate that we would be brought back together again, my brother!"

Sasume said as he reached me and took me into a hug. "your mate? How is this possible? I thought you were still visiting in America; when did you leave America?" I asked. "That my friend was a while back, maybe six months ago?"

"I am only missing Aki now." She said to Shirou, and he looked down at her with so much love that it nearly made my heart melt, then that's when I felt like a ton of bricks hit my head.

Looking to the door, I see the most gorgeous girl walk through it. She looked up at me and didn't look away. Her cute mouth dropped open as she moved closer to me, not even blinking.

As she reached me, everything else seemed to drop away. Nothing else existed. She brought her hands up and softly touched my cheek as I felt like energy was being sapped from me.

I gently placed my hand over hers and couldn't look away from her soft brown eyes that had flecks of gold in them. When she finally spoke, sounding nearly as clear as wind chimes, "mate."

••Luna Willard••

I was pretty surprised when Jeremy had said that we were going on a trip to Japan. Knowing that he had an agenda, I didn't question it; it was when my son and brother were acting secretive that it started bothering me.

I had a longing to see my daughter even though she had her own family for twenty years now; I have felt such guilt for letting her go.

I was just scared for Zachery and what was left of our Pack after the attack of the witches. She had too much power and unnatural skills since birth. I kept in touch with the Takeda family after they adopted her.

I could see the joy in Zachery's face as we walked onto the plane, it was a long fight, but I was relieved when we arrived at our last departure.

The drive was pleasant and quiet; I looked at the gorgeous scenery as we drove through the wooded area; it was really serene. We drove through tall, decorated gates; the children were playing kickball.

They were yelling and laughing, running passed the car. I barely notice my son leaving the vehicle in a hurry, then caught the sight of a small woman jump on him. I got out of the car quickly then felt Jeremy behind me holding me tight, probably thinking I would do something rash; I drew in a sharp breath witch my so had heard as he turned to look at me in my mate's arms.

He was smiling with tears forming in his eyes. I let out a soft sigh, now feeling more guilt than ever. Seeing him reunited with his sister is something else entirely. Some of the council had looked down at my choices of separating them at birth as I did. Some of them told me that they were surprised that he even lived with being separated the way he was from her.

One of the many reasons I had asked the Takeda family to stay in America a year passed what they had initially been planned to visit. Snuggled into my mate's arms, I closed my eyes for a moment while they got reacquainted.

I didn't want to disrupt them; they needed this. Jeremy has been there for me and has taken in the broken family and turned into something intense and unbreakable.

It seems as though he is still fixing us whether I am ready for it or not, ever the opportunist. He is definitely the love of my life, my second chance as I was to him.

I was when I see another mate of hers coming out, and I realize that he was one of Zachery's old friends that he made when the young man came down to visit during some schooling or something like that.

Then a cute girl came out and froze, staring at Zachery then sauntering. I have seen that look that she had given him.

I was so ecstatic she is his mate; finally, my boy has found his family and his other half.

We were shown to our rooms in the main manor; it was very quaint, lightly decorated, futons rolled and pushed to the side near the closet.

After we dropped our things off in the room, we returned to the kitchen; that's when I felt a hand rest on my arm with a beautiful woman looking at me; it was like looking in a time capsule back at myself.

"Could you spare a moment with me, Luna?" She said in a soft voice, still very rich in a Japanese accent. I smiled at the politeness this child was showing me even after knowing who I was and obviously what I had done.

However, I am not sure if she knows why I had felt the need to do it. I was hoping she wouldn't think too terribly of me and think I was a bad person who threw her away.

We walked into what looked like a sitting room; it had just chairs and small tables with vases of orchids and other orient flowers.

Each of us sitting next to each other, she began to ask me questions with curiosity rather than animosity; I was relieved that she believed me that what I did was probably the right choice with the circumstances; the Takedas really brought her up with love, and for that I was grateful.

We talked about the rape, not in detail, but enough for her to understand, as well as losing my first love, my mate, and that I was so lucky to find a second mate. I explained that I did keep tabs on her finding out that she was one remarkable woman. She would nod her head in understanding and tried not to ask too many things on the sensitive subjects. When we were done talking, I knew she would never see me as a mom, but we were closer now. I will take that as many steps forward.

 Mitsuki's mates walked in; she smiled brightly and introduced them to me; they were so polite, from what she told me, I wasn't wrong about her being a witch, but she also had a fox and a wolf. That explained the three mates, what a handful; I don't think I could have handled three of them, but they really seemed to love her and work well together since they were all brothers. I figured it was a bit strange. As long as she was happy and they were happy, I guess that is all that matters in the end.

We all had dinner together with the Takeda and Naito family with all of us here. I could see how my family had grown; it was so lovely. I could see a little of the future now; small children will be running all over the place. Everything seemed so right until a loud siren rang out.

The three Alphas stood up abruptly and left the room as my son, and Mitsuki's mates gathered my son's mate Giana, Mitsuki, Luna Takeda, and me to a safe room. Everything was in a panic. I asked if the other families had places to go, and Shirou had said they would be fine. Mitsuki's eyes had turned purple suddenly, and she stood up, shoving her mates and brother out of the way, leaving the room and locking it behind her keeping us locked in the safe room. "I have to go. You stay here; they don't want you." is all she said as we heard her running out of the manor, the door slamming behind her. I looked to her mates, wondering what the hell they were doing still standing there, all the men looked at me in fear. "We can't move!! My son screamed.

Not Quite The End,

To be continued…

ABOUT THE AUTHOR

Colleen Sanchez lives in South Texas with her children, husband, and lovely Papillons that she shows with the family. She enjoys traveling to new places; when not working on her own stories, she's diving into paranormal romance novels and spending time with her little dogs and children.

~ *Colleen Sanchez*